It's Called Solari

A Rock, a Scar, and a Search for Truth

Tommy Turner

It's Called Solari
A Rock, a Scar, and a Search for Truth

ISBN 978-1-954269-06-4

Dedication

To my sister, Georgina— and to the friends whose words helped me find my voice.

Author's Note

This book is for the ones who have lost something they can't name, who keep walking even when the road disappears. It's for the ones who have prayed with cracked voices, who have begged for clarity and gotten silence—but kept going anyway, still searching for why they're here.

It's for those who wonder if their pain disqualifies them, who need to hear that it doesn't.

I wrote this because I believe in hopeful stories—the kind that help people believe again. The kind that remind the forgotten they are not forgotten. This isn't just a book. It's my offering. My calling. A way to say: You are seen. You are not alone. And you still have a purpose.

Contents

Reflection 1

Introduction 3

1   The First Rock 5

2   Wordless Prayer 9

3   Warmth from Within 15

4   Alive and Waiting 19

5   No Simple Answers 25

6   The Morning Walk 31

7   A Silhouette 39

8   Marked Long Ago 45

9   The Echo of Familiar 51

10 Mornings Like This 57

11 The Way It Starts 63

12 More Than a Story 69

13 A Stranger Remembered 77

14 A Voice Returning 83

15 The Turning Point 87

16 Not Just a Story 93

17 The Scars We Carry 99

18 Chapters Without Endings 107

19 The Feeling's Mutual 113

20 The Words We Carry 119

21 When the Scar Speaks 125

22 The Manuscript 131

23 The Unexpected Lunch Break 139

24 Time to Go Back 145

25 The Restless Room 151

26 The Unexplainable Moment 157

27 Toward the Hill 163

28 The Hill Called Skull 169

29 The Weight that Remained 175

30 Final Resting Place 183

31 The Ending He Knew 187

32 The Confirmation 191

33 The Final Stretch 197

34 What Remains 201

35 The Call from Home 207

36 The Final Touches 213

37 Before the Verdict 217

38 Give It Time 221

39 Ben's Story 227

Reflection

I don't know if I chose this story or if it chose me. I only know that it kept stirring and tugging until I said yes.

Much of what you'll find here began as questions—unanswered ones. I didn't set out to write a book about a scarred rock, a quiet man, a romance, or a vision of Jesus. I set out looking for something I couldn't quite name: peace, maybe. Or presence. Or just the quiet hope that I'm walking in what I was made to do.

Writing has always been about release—about pouring out what's inside, even if no one reads it. Even if no one claps. That's why I believe this story matters. Not because it's perfect. But because it's offered.

So, if you're reading this book, thank you. Thank you for opening this book. For making room in your life, even briefly, for mine. I hope you find something within these pages that lingers. A scar that heals. A whisper that stays. A truth that defines.

I don't have all the answers. But I believe the One Who began a good work in me is still carrying it toward completion. And maybe, if these pages mean anything to you, then that good work is still unfolding—in both of us.

With all my heart,
Tommy Turner

Introduction

I didn't set out to write a book like this. At first, I was just trying to process some pain—to make sense of the past. But somewhere along the way, the story shifted. It stopped being about what I'd lost and became about what I'd been given.

I found myself writing not to be understood, but to bear witness—to truth, to grace, to something sacred that broke through in silence and stayed.

The man in this story isn't perfect. He's marked, searching, and a little lost—maybe like you, maybe like me. But he's learning—slowly, painfully—how to let go of control and lean into something deeper. Something holy.

I don't know how many people this story will reach. That part isn't up to me. I only knew I couldn't keep it in.

One thought kept returning as I wrote, and I suppose it's what carried me to the end:

I'd rather write a story that's never read than bury a story that's never written.

That's why this book exists.

Not for noise. Not for numbers. But because some stories won't let you go—until you let them out.

Ben's story is for you.

CHAPTER 1

The First Rock

Ben Thomas hadn't retired, exactly. He'd just stopped showing up to the parts of life that weren't honest anymore. He still took on a piano gig here and there and traded stocks most mornings—more for rhythm than for wealth—but the days of packed calendars and late-night obligations had faded.

What replaced them wasn't rest. Not really. It was more like space. And with that space came silence. And with the silence, questions.

Sometimes he thought back to the long nights backstage—quiet moments tucked between spotlight and darkness—where he'd shared stories and meals with legends. Not just performers, but icons. The kind of names etched into vinyl and memory. Some were kind, some troubled, some barely holding it together—but all unforgettable. Some were gone now, passed on like old songs no longer played. Yet their voices lingered in him, woven into the soundtrack of his life.

He wouldn't call it sadness. Not even regret. Just a steady ache—low in the chest, hard to name, easy to ignore until the noise died down and nowhere was left to hide. It was the feeling that life, for all its motion, had somehow drifted off course. That somewhere along the way, he'd missed something. Or maybe everything.

He'd always enjoyed writing. Mostly in journals—unfiltered, unpolished. Pages that reached for comfort or clawed for clarity. His laptop held years of files: scattered thoughts and half-finished ideas that never quite landed. They circled something. They wandered. But they never found a home.

Ben had self-published a few nonfiction books over the years—quiet reflections stitched together from lived moments, journal pages, and midnight thoughts. A few dozen readers here and there. Maybe they helped someone. Maybe not. But even in the writing, he sensed they were fragments—shards of something truer he hadn't yet found. Like trying to describe a song by humming a single note. The real story—the one that mattered—still hovered just beyond reach, waiting for words he didn't yet have.

At sixty-five, Ben wasn't trying to write about life anymore. He wanted to write from it. From something honest. Something weighty. Something he could hold in his hands and say, "This is true." That's what brought him here. To the edge of everything.

Ilwaco.

Decades ago, he'd been to this small, weathered town at the southern corner of Washington State, where the Columbia River slides into the Pacific. The memory was more sensation than details—a gray sky, the tang of salt, a sense of something ending or beginning; he wasn't sure which. But lately, Ilwaco had kept surfacing in his mind, quiet and persistent, like a tide rising beneath the surface.

He didn't fight it. He packed lightly—his laptop, a few notebooks, and a quiet hope that maybe this was it. Not a polished plan. Not a grand mission. Just the fragile sense that something had been stirring for a long time, and now it might finally speak.

He arrived on a Tuesday under a sky that looked like pewter. Fog drifted low across the harbor, blurring the edges of boats and buildings. The air smelled like driftwood and seaweed and the ghost of something older. He parked at the edge of town, stepped out of his Corvette, and stood for a moment with the door open, letting the quiet settle over him.

No one was around—only seagulls in the distance, circling something unseen. He closed the door gently, slid a notebook under his arm, and walked.

He didn't need directions. The ocean is always called from the same place. The path was uneven, lined with wind-bent trees and patches of grass that never fully dried. When he reached the sand, he paused, kicked off his shoes, and let the cold Pacific water wrap around his ankles. It stung—but in a good way. The kind of sting that says *you're still here.*

He breathed in. Salt. Distance. A trace of cedar from somewhere inland.

The questions rose almost immediately. Not new ones. Familiar ones that had never quite gone away.

God, do You still speak?

Am I doing this right?

Do you still have something left for me to do?

He didn't expect answers. But asking felt right. Like turning soil after a long frost.

He reached down and picked up a rock—smooth, gray, heavier than it looked. This one was rougher than most, cool to the touch, with a few shallow lines crossing its surface.

He turned it once in his palm, then slipped it into his pocket.

He walked on, barefoot and slow, the morning breeze cool against his skin.

The tide moved without urgency. So did he.

CHAPTER 2

Wordless Prayer

He used to think silence meant peace—stillness, clarity, the uncluttering of noise. But now, the silence felt heavier. It didn't clear things out; it pressed inward, like fog against glass. It made the space inside him echo, and that echo had a voice. Not loud, but constant—whispering the same questions he'd pushed aside for years, hoping they'd lose strength if ignored long enough.

They hadn't.

Ilwaco wasn't a place he'd ever planned to return to. It had barely registered the first time—just a quiet town on the edge of the map, where the Columbia met the Pacific. But now, with the ache in his chest sharper than it used to be and the road ahead narrowing, Ilwaco called to him—not with answers, but with quiet.

And sometimes, that was enough.

The motel was nothing special—two tired stories of damp carpet and peeling trim, just close enough to the beach to smell the sea through a cracked window. He hadn't come for charm or comfort. He came because everywhere else felt wrong. And because this place—like him—had a past. Some of it good. Some of it broken.

The faded sign creaked with each gust off the water. The parking lot always looked half-abandoned. Lonely.

But it faced west. That mattered.

Each morning, he rose before the sky gave any hint of light, dressed in silence, grabbed a cup of weak motel coffee from the lobby, and stepped into the gray. The wind met him early, brushing past like it had someplace to be, carrying the familiar scents of salt and pine and something metallic—like rust, or memory. The path to the beach was little more than a rutted trail through dune grass and driftwood piles, with a fence that leaned more with each passing year.

The sea had drawn back, leaving behind a rippled canvas of wet earth, seaweed, and driftwood scattered like the remnants of a shipwrecked dream. Small rivulets of water twisted and turned across the beach, carving lazy paths back toward the waves—like veins feeding an invisible heart.

The beach stretched wide and empty—the kind of empty that didn't ask to be filled. Just sand, sea, and the steady rhythm of waves tumbling and retreating like breath. Ben moved without hurrying, boots crunching across the wet sand, one hand in his jacket pocket, the other curled loosely around the coffee cup.

He didn't pray. At least, not in words. He didn't ask questions, either—not directly. But the questions walked with him as silent companions in the corners of his mind.

Sometimes, without thinking, he bent to pick up a stone.

It was something he'd done for years—maybe decades. Never planned, never explained. Just a quiet pull toward certain shapes, certain weights. Smooth ones, mostly. Stones that fit his palm like they'd been waiting for it.

By now, he'd collected hundreds. Most sat quietly on shelves back home, reminders of past walks by the sea. A few were still tucked inside jacket pockets, like old receipts from days that didn't ask for proof.

He never named them. Never sorted them. It wasn't about that. It was simple. Grounding. A habit that felt like prayer without words.

Breadcrumbs, maybe. Markers of where he'd been. A way to keep from losing the path entirely.

He spotted one just ahead, half-buried in wet sand—gray, flecked with a line of white across the top. He crouched and picked it up, turning it over in his hand. It wasn't perfect; nothing he kept ever was. He liked that. He slid it into his pocket and moved on.

A little farther down, he found a smaller one—smooth and dark, shaped like a tear, flattened by time. He paused, rubbed his thumb across the surface, then added it to the others. A few yards beyond that, a wider, flatter stone—cool to the touch and pocked with faint dimples, like it had been chewed by the sea, presented itself.

He didn't look for them. They just showed up. And most days, that felt like enough.

By the time he reached the tide line, his coffee had cooled, but he didn't mind. A crab shell lay cracked in half near a clump of kelp—everything broken by the tide seemed to wash up eventually. A seagull strutted in tight circles near a driftwood pile, pecking at something unseen. He watched it for a while, then turned back toward the dunes.

He paused once more, stooping to pick up one last rock before heading in. This one was darker than the others, almost black when wet. He held it loosely, turned it twice in his hand, then tucked it away with the rest.

It didn't need to be special. It just needed to be real. Something the ocean had shaped and left behind.

He walked slowly back toward the motel, the morning still dim, the sky still undecided. The rocks clicked gently in his pocket with each step. He didn't think much of it. That was the point. He wasn't here to understand anything—not yet. Just to be still. Just to walk. Just to listen.

He said nothing aloud the whole way back—just heard the seagulls in the distance and the steady breath of the sea rolling out behind him.

He'd come to the coast for quiet.

And the quiet, for now, was enough.

Tomorrow, he'd probably do the same thing.

And maybe, one of these days, he'd start writing again.

But not today.

CHAPTER 3

Warmth from Within

Ben didn't check the time. The light outside had shifted—just enough to stir him from sleep into movement. He dressed in the quiet, layering his clothes like armor; poured the last of the motel coffee into his thermos; and stepped out into the cold.

The morning was damp and still. Fog lay low across the gravel lot, blurring the edges of cars, signs, and sky. A faint breath of salt hung in the air, laced with pine and something metallic, like the scent of rusted memory. He zipped his jacket halfway, tucked the thermos under his arm, and headed down the narrow path through the dunes.

The trail was familiar now—brush along both sides, a leaning fence surrendering to the wind, sand already clinging to his boots before he reached the shore. The tide had pulled back farther than usual. Wide flats of wet sand gleamed under a layered sky, streaked with pale light trying and failing to become sun.

He walked without purpose. Not aimless, but not searching either. His footsteps left soft prints behind him, shallow and temporary, erased within minutes by wind or tide. This walk wasn't about finding anything. It never had been.

His eyes moved across the sand—unfocused, relaxed. Just watching.

Now and then, something would catch his eye—a shape, a weight, a stillness. He never knew why, only that some stones weren't meant to be left behind.

That's why he almost missed it.

Just a shadow of a shape at first—dark, half-buried near the edge of the tide, nestled where the waves had recently passed. It didn't catch the light. It didn't shine. But something about the way it sat—firm, quiet, untouched—made him stop.

He crouched, one knee pressing into the cold sand, and reached for it.

His fingers brushed away the grit. And as he lifted it into his hand, he felt it.

It was warm, but not the kind of warmth left by sun. The sand had been cold. The air was colder still. But the rock—this rock—held a steady, unmistakable warmth that came from within. Not a pulse. Not heat in the way of fire or friction. But presence. Settled. Alive.

It didn't alarm him. But it held him.

He turned it over in his palm slowly, adjusting his grip without thinking.

That's when he saw the scar.

A single arc curved gently along one side—pale and clean. Not hidden. Not dramatic. But seen. Immediately. It didn't call for attention, but it carried something. A weight. A stillness. The kind of mark that remembered pain—and had made peace with it.

The scar held him. Quiet, yes—but certain. Etched with purpose, not by accident. Not jagged. Not rough. Just...there.

His thumb slowly found the groove, traced it. It caught slightly—just enough to be felt. The kind of line carved not to decorate, but to remember.

He stayed like that for a long moment, kneeling in the cold sand, one hand cradling the stone, the other pressed to the ground for balance. The beach stretched wide behind him, but he didn't turn. Didn't move. Didn't want to break whatever this encounter was.

The rock was otherwise unremarkable—gray, smooth, rounded but not polished—about the size of his palm. No glittering minerals. No strange shape. But it held. Not just in his hand, but in the air. In the moment.

It felt like it had waited for this. For him.

He looked up. The ocean was still speaking in slow breaths. The seagulls had gone quiet. Even the wind seemed to pause at his back.

He didn't try to explain it. He didn't need to.

He stood slowly, brushed the cold sand from his knee, and slipped the rock into his jacket pocket. It clicked softly against another. He barely noticed the sound but felt the shift.

Most rocks, he left behind. A few made it to windowsills or shelves. None had felt like this one.

It didn't feel like something he'd collected.

It felt like something that had found him.

He walked a little farther down the shoreline, trying not to hold onto the moment too tightly. But it stayed. Not clinging. Not pressing. Just present. Like the warmth of the rock had bled into the space around him.

He paused once more before turning back toward the motel.

The sky had lightened but not cleared. The fog had lifted just enough to suggest a horizon. It didn't feel like the end of something. It didn't feel like the beginning either.

It felt like a door.

Not open. Not closed. Just...waiting.

Ben walked slowly back up the path, each step sending a soft clatter of stones beneath his feet, the loose rocks shifting and clicking against one another.

He didn't know what this moment meant.

But he knew it meant something.

CHAPTER 4

Alive and Waiting

He hadn't meant to sit so long.

The motel room had dimmed while he sat there, staring at the rock. Not thinking. Not moving. Just watching—the way you watch a fire when there's nothing left to say.

It sat where he'd left it—on the little round table near the window, lit by fading afternoon through salt-blurred glass.

It should've been like the others—just another smooth stone—picked up and forgotten. The kind that show up without searching. Half-buried. Waiting. He'd taken them home, dropped them in bowls, placed them on shelves. Most he forgot.

But this one was different; it still held warmth.

He'd been back from the beach for nearly two hours, and it hadn't cooled. Not completely. Not like it should have. It wasn't hot. Just…steady. Like a pulse. Not loud. Not dramatic. But there.

Like something alive and waiting.

He hadn't planned to write anything, but somewhere between staring and not blinking, he found himself at the desk, notebook open, pen in hand, a line scribbled across the top of the page:

It doesn't feel like a rock. It feels like a reminder.

He didn't know what he meant by it. A reminder of what? There wasn't an answer. But the words lingered. He couldn't bring himself to cross them out. Something in their rhythm felt like it had come from deeper than thought.

Ben finally stood, knees stiff, and slid the notebook closed. He took one last look at the rock before slipping on his jacket and stepping outside. He left it where it was. He didn't think about why that mattered—until he was halfway to the dunes.

The air had cooled slightly, the sky turning to that mid-evening tone where it couldn't decide whether to hold the day or let it go. Fog lingered at the edge of the tree line— just thin enough to soften the world. He moved slowly down the trail, hands shoved deep in his jacket pockets, the faint smell of pine mixing with salt and something older—damp wood, distant rain, time itself. His boots made a dull sound against the path, muted by sand.

He wasn't in a hurry. He didn't have a destination. It was more like the room had become too still, and something in him needed to move through air again.

When he reached the beach, he felt a pull. He didn't walk left as he had earlier. He turned right.

The rock was still on his mind.

It's just a normal rock, he tried to convince himself. *Nothing more.*

But as he continued, creation put on a show—like a child in a first-grade play, eager to be noticed. The light shimmered low across the wet sand, casting everything in that brief hour when shadows stop mattering. His steps were slow, thoughtful, but his mind wasn't at rest.

He kept seeing that scar—the way it curved, not jagged, not accidental. He remembered how his thumb had paused there without being told to. It wasn't a crack. It felt deliberate. A mark that didn't break the stone—but gave it purpose.

He walked a long stretch in silence. A few seagulls moved near the waterline but didn't call. The waves rolled in a little heavier than the day before.

He stopped beside a cluster of stones, half-buried, wet and gleaming. He crouched, touched them one by one—cool to the skin, but not the same. No warmth. No strange familiarity. He stood, dusted his hands, and moved on.

There was no story to find here. No pattern. No mystical energy field.

Just a stretch of coastline and a man who, for reasons he couldn't explain, couldn't stop thinking about something that should've meant nothing.

But it wouldn't let go, sitting in his memory like a line from a song he hadn't heard in years—but still knew every word.

As he walked, he realized he was listening—not to the waves or the birds, but to the silence between them. He wasn't expecting a voice. It wasn't like that. But something in him had turned—tuned to a frequency he hadn't known was there.

It wasn't fear. It wasn't anticipation.

It was presence.

A strange alertness. The kind of stillness you don't notice until it notices you.

The hairs on his arms rose—not from cold, but from awareness.

He walked for nearly an hour. Eventually, the light gave way to dusk, and the horizon folded into itself. He turned back. The fog had crept closer now—not heavy, but enough to give the dunes a shadowed softness. The wind picked up slightly, brushing across his collar.

For a moment, he could almost feel the rock again—its warmth, its weight—even though it was still on the table in his motel room.

The sensation startled him more than he expected. Not because it felt mystical.

But because it felt familiar.

Like a memory that hadn't happened yet.

Back at the motel, he unlocked the door without thinking. The rock sat where he'd left it—unchanged, untouched. He walked past it into the kitchenette, poured a glass of water with a shaky hand, and leaned against the counter.

He didn't believe in magic. He didn't believe in objects holding power.

But something had shifted.

And no matter how ordinary the day had been, he could no longer pretend that what he'd found was just a rock.

CHAPTER 5

No Simple Answers

The morning light found Ben already stirring. Not startled—just done sleeping.

The motel was dim and quiet. A faint edge of blue-gray light pushed against the curtains like morning wasn't quite ready to arrive. For a few minutes, he lay there, eyes open, listening to the silence.

The rock sat on the small round table near the window.

He hadn't touched it since yesterday. It hadn't moved. It shouldn't have changed. And yet, as he stepped out of bed and passed it on the way to the coffee pot, he still felt that quiet warmth. Not heat—just something steady. Familiar. Like a pilot light that never quite went out.

The motel coffee was exactly what he had expected—bitter, weak, barely drinkable—but it was hot, and it gave him something to do while the day slowly took shape.

He opened his laptop on the bed and started typing:

Warm beach rock. Scarred stone. Why does a rock feel alive?

The search results were predictable. New Age blogs. Healing crystals. Forums about energy vibrations and emotional grounding. None of it fit. His rock didn't hum. It didn't sparkle or change color. It just sat there—still, silent, present. A stone with a scar and a quiet kind of weight.

He dug deeper. Geology pages. Scientific threads about igneous rock, sea glass, pressure fractures, thermal retention. Nothing explained what he was holding—or what he was feeling.

Eventually, he gave up and left the motel.

The town was just beginning to wake up. Windows unlocking. Trash cans dragged to the curb. A seagull shrieked overhead. The air smelled like wet wood, diesel, and coffee grounds. He walked without a plan, passing faded storefronts and signs that looked like they hadn't been repainted since the sixties.

He stopped in a small bookstore tucked beside a shop selling wind chimes and shells. Inside, it smelled like dust and soft spine glue. An older man behind the counter was working a crossword puzzle and didn't look up.

Ben wandered the shelves. He wasn't sure what he was hoping for—maybe a folk tale, some regional myth, anything that might offer a clue—but nothing stood out. Finally, he stepped to the counter.

"Hey," he said. "Can I ask you something odd?"

The man glanced up, mildly curious. "Sure."

"You ever hear of people finding rocks on the beach that feel...different? Not shaped weird—warm."

The man leaned back slightly. "You mean like lava rock? Tourist junk?"

Ben shook his head. "No. Just...different. I found one yesterday. Doesn't feel like the others I've picked up."

"Hm," the man said, noncommittal. "People find strange stuff all the time. Sometimes it's the thing. Sometimes it's the person."

Ben nodded. "Right."

That was all. No stories. No advice. Just a man doing his crossword.

He left the bookstore and kept walking.

The rest of the day passed in fragments. He browsed in a thrift store without really looking. Sat at a café and watched people come and go. Bought a sandwich and ate it at a harbor picnic table, seagulls circling like they had nowhere better to be.

It was evening before he realized how long he'd been out. His legs ached a little, and the wind had picked up. He found a diner—quiet, nothing flashy, a hand-lettered menu in the window—and stepped inside. A bell on the door jingled. A few older couples sat in booths, eating slowly, saying little.

He slid into a booth near the window. The waitress brought him water and a menu without a smile—but not unfriendly either. Just tired. Like someone who'd been on her feet too long.

He ordered coffee, a bowl of chowder, and a grilled cheese sandwich. Comfort food. Something familiar.

He didn't mean to pull the rock from his pocket, but as he sat there with his coffee, turning the mug in his hands, he found himself holding it again. He set it on the table beside the spoon.

When the waitress returned to refill his coffee, she paused mid-pour. Her eyes caught on the rock.

"Where'd you find that one?" she asked, curiosity flickering in her voice.

Ben looked up. "Down on the beach. Just off the north trail."

She reached out and picked it up without asking. As soon as it touched her palm, she stopped. Turned it over. Her brow furrowed.

"Huh?" she said. "That's… weird. It's warm." She ran her thumb slowly over the surface. Then she stopped. "And this mark—almost looks like it was carved."

He nodded. "Yeah. I know."

She looked at him now, genuinely intrigued. "What is it?"

"I don't know," Ben said. "Just a rock, I think. But…not like the others."

She handed it back slowly. "No kidding. I've picked up a lot of beach stuff. Never felt anything like that." She finished pouring the coffee, but her eyes stayed on the rock like she wasn't quite sure if she imagined it.

Ben slid it back into his pocket.

She lingered another second. "There's an old guy walks the beach here most mornings. Has for years. Forty, I think someone said. One of those regulars that people stop seeing. But he might know something. You'd have to catch him early."

"Thanks," Ben said.

She smiled—not much, just a crease at the corner of her mouth. "Hope you find what you're looking for. Whatever that is."

He nodded, unsure what to say.

Back at the motel, he turned off the lights and settled into bed. The glow from the parking lot filtered through the curtain, just like the night before, and fell across the table.

The rock sat in its usual place.

Still. Silent.

But holding something.

CHAPTER 6

The Morning Walk

Morning came early, but this time it brought a sense of direction.

The room was cold, darker than the day before. The curtains were still drawn, letting only a faint gray smear leak through at the edges. The hum of the mini-fridge, the subtle creak of the walls adjusting to the cold, and the distant sigh of the ocean—all folded around him like a reminder: *You're not home, but you're here.*

He moved slowly—not because he was tired, but because the silence gave him room to think. He dressed without turning on the lights, one layer at a time, methodical and quiet. His jacket was still draped over the chair. He reached for it, paused, then turned back to the table.

The rock was there—same as ever, waiting without urgency. It hadn't shifted. It hadn't cooled. It still held that impossible warmth—not from sun, or touch, or room temperature. A steady presence. One that didn't press itself on him but also didn't let go.

He cupped it in his hands for a moment before slipping it gently into his pocket.

Outside, the town hadn't quite woken up. Porchlights flickered faintly but most windows remained dark. He passed a bakery just beginning to stir, the smell of yeast and something sweet trailing behind him. A few cars moved through the fog—slow, deliberate, unhurried.

Ben headed for the shoreline toward the trail that led to the north beach—the place the waitress had pointed him toward the night before.

He didn't know what he expected. And maybe that was the point.

He wasn't chasing a miracle or hoping for an explanation. He simply needed to follow the thread. Sometimes that's all you have—one thread that doesn't break when everything else feels like it's unraveling.

The sand was cold beneath his shoes, still dark in places where the tide had recently receded. The beach was wide, empty, and quiet except for the hush of waves and the distant call of seagulls. A man in a flannel coat walked a shepherd near the dunes. A woman jogged by, her earbuds tucked in, eyes straight ahead.

Nobody looked at him. That was fine.

Ben walked a long time. Long enough for the cold to settle along the backs of his arms. Long enough for the noise in his head to quiet. He wasn't here for a sign. He just wanted to know if the old man was real—or if the previous night's conversation had been a gentle bit of fiction.

And then he saw him.

Far ahead, near the curve of the beach where the dunes sloped down and the driftwood piled, an older man walked alone. He moved with practiced rhythm—measured but purposeful. Not like someone passing time, but someone using it. He wore a faded yellow raincoat that flapped slightly in the wind, and black boots that left clear impressions on the wet sand. His hands were in his coat pockets. His head was slightly bowed.

Ben approached slowly, careful not to disrupt the rhythm. When he was close enough, he spoke.

"Morning."

The man looked over, not startled—just aware. He gave a slow nod. "Morning."

Ben fell in beside him, not quite shoulder to shoulder. "Hope I'm not interrupting."

"Not unless you're here to take the ocean from me," the man said, with a dry edge to his voice.

"I heard you walk this stretch most mornings."

"That's right. Been doing it since before my knees started complaining about it. It's how I talk to God—and if I'm quiet enough, how I listen to Him talk back. This stretch is quieter than church, and He doesn't seem to mind the wind."

They walked a few steps in silence before Ben spoke again.

"I found something here the other day. Just off the north trail. It's probably nothing, but I can't stop thinking about it"

He reached into his jacket and pulled out the rock. It looked smaller now. Less mysterious. But no less present.

The man accepted it without hesitation, like this wasn't the first time someone handed him something strange. But when it touched his palm, he paused.

"It's warm," he said, glancing up. Not surprised—just observing.

Ben nodded.

The man turned the rock over slowly. "This mark—you feel it more than see it. Old, but still clear. Like it held onto something long after it was done being shaped."

Ben waited.

"It's seen some wear," the man added. "Tumbled long enough to lose its edges, but not long enough to forget where it's been wounded. That scar—that's not random."

"You ever seen anything like it?"

"Can't say I have," the man replied, brushing his thumb along the curve. "I've found plenty of strange things. Driftwood shaped like animals. Bottles with notes inside. Rocks with faces. This one's different, sure. But it's a beach. You find things. Most folks just don't keep them."

Ben nodded. "Just wanted to know if it stood out."

"Maybe," the man said. "Hard to tell what matters and what doesn't out here."

Ben hesitated, then asked, "You said you walk to listen. Do you ever hear anything?"

The man smiled. A crease formed at the edge of his eye. "Sometimes. But mostly I hear myself—until the ocean gets loud enough to drown me out. That's when I figure God's trying to get through."

They stood quietly for a while, both looking out over the surf.

"There's a place," the man said eventually. "Down in Lincoln City. South end of town. Rock shop called *Windward Stones.* Been around a long time. I don't know if they'll give you any answers, but they know rocks better than most people know themselves. If there's something to learn, it might start there."

Ben thanked him. They shook hands. The man continued walking without another word.

By the time Ben got back to the motel, the town had fully awakened. He sat at the small table, opened his laptop, and typed:

Windward Stones – Est. 1972. Closed today. Open tomorrow at 10:00 a.m.

He leaned back and looked around the room. Then out the window.

Ilwaco had been good to him. Quiet. Grounding. *But I'm not here just to stand still.*

Not anymore.

That evening, he returned to the diner. Same booth. Same waitress. This time, he noticed her name: Jill.

She smiled when she saw him. "Thought you might show up."

"Yeah," he said. "Figured I'd get one last meal before I head out."

"Find the old guy?"

"Found him. Good man. Sent me south—rock shop in Lincoln City. Said it might be worth a stop."

She filled his coffee and glanced at the table. "You still have it?"

Ben smirked. "You're curious."

"Aren't you?"

He pulled the rock from his pocket and placed it on the table.

Jill didn't touch it right away. She just looked at it, as if waiting for it to shift. Then she reached out and held it in both hands, her fingers folding gently around it.

Her eyes closed—not dramatically. Just a quiet beat.

When she opened them again, she said softly, "This rock has something."

Ben didn't reply. Just took it back when she handed it over.

She smiled as she refilled his cup. "Hope you find what you're after."

After dinner, Ben walked the town one last time. The windows were warm with light. The sidewalks still uneven.

He passed the bait shop, the bookstore, and the bench where he'd sat the day before.

Everything looked the same.

But something in him had shifted. Not a lot, but just enough.

At the edge of the beach, he stood still for a long while, jacket zipped high, hands in his pockets. The ocean spoke the way it always had—slow, patient, ancient. The rock rested quietly in his coat, warm as ever. Not louder. Just there.

When the cold finally found its way through the seams of his collar and touched his spine, he turned and walked back to the motel.

Inside, he set the rock on the table, pulled out his notebook, and opened a blank page.

At the top, he wrote: *What have I found?*

Then paused. Crossed it out.

Underneath, he wrote: *No…what has found me?*

He stared at the words for a long time. Then, slowly, he began to write.

Would God use a rock to speak to me? Why not just speak? Why not something louder? Or maybe He already has. Maybe this is what it sounds like when I finally go quiet enough to listen.

He let the pen rest in the fold of the notebook.

Then he stood, turned out the light, and went to bed.

Tomorrow, I will head south.

CHAPTER 7

A Silhouette

Ben didn't look back when he left Ilwaco.

No dramatic pause. No lingering glance at the motel window. No final gesture to mark the end of anything. Just the soft click of the door, the drag of the zipper on his bag, and a quiet breath—as if he'd packed something uncertain alongside his clothes.

There was no weight of visions. No collapse. Just a steady curiosity he hadn't felt in years.

The Corvette came alive with a low, confident growl. Ben slid behind the wheel and paused, his hands resting at ten and two like a man waiting for clearance to taxi. Outside, the morning light pressed through fog in soft bands. The gravel lot shimmered with damp quiet. He didn't rush. Just let the engine idle, let the silence stretch. Let the feeling settle.

Something inside him had decided to move—even if it didn't yet know where to land.

He pulled onto Highway 101 just as the first blush of dawn touched the tops of the trees. The road unwound southward, hugging the coast like it had something to say—if you were quiet enough to listen. Fog drifted low over the cliffs, brushing the pines with soft gray fingers. The hum of the tires and the rhythm of the curves brought a calm he hadn't realized he needed.

The ocean came and went beside him—sometimes hidden, sometimes wide open. Always steady. Always there. It didn't ask questions. It just moved.

He passed through small towns—Hebo, Cloverdale, Neskowin—without stopping. Places that felt more like rhythm than destination. Sidewalks swept. Coffee brewed. CLOSED signs flipped to OPEN. Life continued. He caught glimpses of it: a kid balancing on a skateboard, a woman walking a limping dog, an old man counting change at a gas station.

Ben wasn't chasing a sign. Just the next step. And today, that step was a rock shop.

Windward Stones. That's what the man on the beach had said. Ben didn't know what he'd find—if anything—but the rock had stirred something in him. Not awe. Not fear. Just a pull. A question. A thread.

He found the shop just past the edge of town, tucked behind a weathered sign and a row of wind-bent pines. If you didn't know it was there, you'd miss it.

He parked, climbed the steps, and felt a quiet hope rise.

Then saw the note taped to the door:

Closed today. Family emergency. Will reopen tomorrow at 10:00 a.m.

Ben stepped back and read it again, as if the words might change. They didn't.

But he didn't feel frustration—just a quiet exhale. He'd come hoping for something. A conversation. A nudge. A thread to follow. Not today.

Still, Lincoln City had always held a kind of calm. Familiar, but not worn out. A place that didn't ask anything from you, but still offered something back. He could wait one more day.

He found a motor lodge perched on a bluff above the beach—the kind of place that didn't advertise. The paint was faded. The sign leaned into the wind. But the view stretched wide into the Pacific.

That was enough.

The woman at the desk handed him a worn key labeled *Room 7.* You don't see many actual keys at motels anymore, but he didn't question it. It just felt right. The number landed inside him with a quiet click. Not a beginning. Not an end. Just…a hinge.

The room was clean, scented faintly with salt and cedar. He flicked on the lights, scanned the space, and turned on the coffeepot. It brewed the usual motel-grade cup—thin, bitter, but hot.

He stepped onto the deck, coffee in hand, and let the day meet him.

The ocean spread wide and gray beneath a sky that hadn't made up its mind. The breeze pressed against his jacket. Salt. Wet wood. Space.

At first, it was just the usual. A seagull overhead. The waves folding and unfolding. The soft hush of a coastline that knew how to wait.

Then he saw her.

A woman—a distant silhouette moving across the sand. But something in her pace caught his attention. Slow. Grounded. Not wandering. Not killing time.

Present.

A long coat swayed around her calves. Her hands were in her pockets. Her head slightly bowed—not in grief, not in defeat, but in reflection.

She wasn't walking for exercise. She wasn't putting on anything. She was simply there—still, even while moving.

Ben watched for a while. Not with purpose. Just curiosity. Something was familiar in the way she stood near the water—like someone who didn't visit the ocean but belonged to it. Like she'd come to listen.

He let his gaze drift, took in the shifting light and the rhythm of the waves. But his attention kept circling back to her.

Not because he knew her. Not because he should.

But because something about her presence felt known.

He didn't try to name it. He just took note.

Later, he walked the beach. The sand was cold beneath his feet, damp and textured. The wind came sharply from the north, flattening the sea into long silver bands. Clouds pressed low on the horizon. The rock in his pocket stayed warm. Still. Steady.

He didn't need answers. Not today.

He just needed motion. The sense of space widening again. The hush returning.

He bought a sandwich from a small café. Wandered a few shops without touching anything. Let the day drift by like seafoam—light, unhurried.

When he returned to the motel, the sun had begun to sink. He stepped onto the deck again with coffee in hand. The breeze carried salt and woodsmoke. Lights blinked on down the boardwalk. A single seagull called, then went quiet.

And then—just to his left, on the next balcony—he saw her.

She'd stepped outside with a mug in one hand, and in the other, a small, smooth rock. The kind you pick up on instinct and never quite let go.

She didn't examine it. Just held it. Like it belonged there.

She didn't seem to notice him. Or if she did, she gave no sign.

Ben didn't stare. But he didn't look away either. A certain stillness in her held the moment just a little longer than it should've lasted. Not staged. Not heavy.

Just honest.

She turned slightly toward the horizon. The ocean breathed.

It wasn't a meeting.

But it felt like the start of something.

Her gaze flicked briefly in his direction—just enough for their eyes to nearly meet—then drifted away again, unhurried.

Ben didn't speak. He wasn't ready to open anything yet.

But something in him shifted. Quietly. Clearly.

He turned back toward the sea and watched the waves roll in.

He didn't know what tomorrow would bring. Maybe the rock shop would offer answers. Maybe not.

Maybe what he needed hadn't been waiting inside the rock.

Maybe it had been waiting inside him.

Tonight, he didn't need to know.

Tonight, it was enough to be here—in this space, in this stillness, in this question that asked nothing and gave everything.

Tomorrow, he'd go to the shop.

CHAPTER 8

Marked Long Ago

Sleep slowly loosened its hold this time with a purpose—not rushed, not anxious, but quietly drawn. For the first time since finding the rock, he felt the pull of forward motion. The air outside his window was still. The tide had pulled out, leaving the beach smooth and quiet, like a slate waiting to be written on.

He dressed simply—a jacket over a long-sleeved shirt, the stone in his pocket like a familiar weight. Not heavy. Not cold. Just steady.

He skipped coffee and breakfast. He wasn't hungry. He was hoping—no, praying—that someone inside that weathered little shop could tell him what this "thing" was. The object that he had, for reasons he still didn't understand, refused to let go.

The walk was short. The storefront looked worn—fogged windows at the corners, peeling paint on the sills, a wind-scuffed sign above the door that read: *Windward Stones.*

It wasn't much to look at. But Ben hadn't come for looks. He came for clarity.

A small wooden plaque by the entrance read: **Open. Welcome.**

Ben stepped inside.

A tired bell rang overhead. The air smelled of cedar and salt. Long glass cases displayed rows of polished agates, geodes cracked open like thunder, fossilized shells, obsidian shards. Light filtered softly through skylights and caught the surfaces of the stones. The place felt like a library, if books had been replaced by the quiet weight of memory.

A woman stood behind the counter—mid-thirties maybe, her ponytail tucked through a faded ballcap, reading from a spiral notebook. She looked up as Ben approached.

"Good morning," she said with warmth. Natural. Not rehearsed.

Ben nodded, reached into his pocket, and set the rock gently on the counter.

Her gaze dropped to it—and stayed. Something shifted in her face. Not alarm. Just a quiet attention. She didn't look up. "Grandpa?" she called, still staring at the stone.

An older man emerged from the back room—stooped a bit, white beard, heavy hands. He moved slowly, but with purpose. The kind of man who had spent a lifetime listening more than speaking.

He leaned over the rock, picked it up, and turned it in his palm.

"Well, I'll be," he said, voice low. "It's been a long time since someone's walked in with one of these."

"What is it?" Ben asked.

The woman gestured toward a shelf behind her. "It's called *Solari.* Latin root. It means 'of the sun' or 'warmed by light.' Known for holding heat—real, steady warmth. Not common around here. But this one…"

She trailed off, then glanced at her grandfather.

"Not many found this far north," the old man added. "My father found one down near Trinidad, California. They're volcanic in origin. Dense enough to trap thermal resonance. You can leave one in the cold overnight, and it'll still feel like it's been sunlit."

He turned the rock slowly. His fingers paused on the scar.

"But this…" he said, brow knitting. "This isn't part of the formation."

The granddaughter pulled a wooden box from the shelf and opened it. Inside was another *Solari*—similar weight and shape, with a faint warmth to it. Smooth, unmarked. Just dimples and variations like melted wax.

The old man nodded toward the box. "That one came from Big Sur. But this mark on yours—that's something else."

Ben leaned in. "What do you mean?"

He held the rock under the light. "See here? That curve. It's not geological. Too precise. Erosion doesn't carve that way."

Ben frowned. "So…someone made it?"

"I'd say so," the man said. "Not decorative. Not recent. But deliberate. And old. Real old."

Ben hesitated. "I've felt something since I found it. Like it's holding more than heat."

The old man chuckled, kindly. "Some rocks do that. Especially ones like this. Some just…carry things. History. Thought. Intention."

Ben gestured to the scar. "But that—why?"

The man shrugged. "That's the mystery. Maybe a settler marked it. Maybe someone tried to leave a message. Could've been a hundred years ago. Maybe more."

The bell above the door rang again.

Ben turned.

It was her.

She stepped in—her coat catching a soft gust before the door clicked shut. For a moment, she paused, her eyes adjusting to the light. The shop hummed—not mechanical, not musical. Just the stillness of old things, arranged with care.

Her gaze drifted.

Then found him.

Ben offered a small smile. "Morning."

"Morning," she said. Her voice, though new to him, felt familiar. She looked at the rock in his hand. "That's a good one. You find it here?"

He shook his head. "Ilwaco. A few days ago."

She stepped closer, curiosity leading. "I don't make it that far north often. But that rock…it's familiar in a strange kind of way. Do you know what it is?"

"Actually, just found out it's called *Solari*. First time I've heard the term."

"Same," she said and smiled. "I've been coming to this stretch of coast for years. I collect sometimes. Some come home with me. Most stay behind."

Ben nodded. "Yeah. I know that rhythm."

He turned the stone once more. "This one, though…I couldn't leave it. Can't explain why."

He looked at her, a quiet openness in his voice. "I saw you yesterday on the beach. And again—on the motel deck. Next balcony down, I think."

She blinked, then smiled. "Oh. Sorry—I didn't notice."

"No reason you should've. But it's nice to meet you. I'm Ben."

She extended her hand. "Claire."

Her grip was light, steady. The kind of handshake that belonged to someone unhurried by time.

"Nice to meet you, Claire."

"You too."

She glanced toward the front window, where a flyer was taped beside the door   colors faded by sun, the edges curling.

Then, casually, "You sticking around long?"

Ben shrugged. "Wasn't planning on it. But this place…I don't know. Something about it."

Claire smiled. "Well—if you are, there's a concert tonight. Josh Avery's playing at Chinook Winds."

Ben blinked. "Josh Avery? That can't be right. I used to gig with Josh. Back in the day—coffeehouses, dive bars. Didn't know he was still performing."

Claire raised an eyebrow. "You're kidding."

Ben laughed. "Nope. Small world."

She gave a quiet nod. "He still plays here every summer. Kind of a tradition now."

Ben looked down at the rock in his hand, then back at her. "Sounds like I'll be sticking around a little longer."

Claire smiled. "Well then…maybe I'll see you there."

Ben returned the smile. "I hope so."

The Echo of Familiar

Ben spent the rest of the afternoon wandering, without aim but not without thought. He ducked into a used bookstore, skimmed a few old titles, grabbed a coffee from a quiet café that smelled like cinnamon and woodsmoke. The sky had cleared a little, the clouds beginning to lift.

He hadn't found what he thought he would. The rock wasn't magical or mythical. But it was rare. And the scar—that was real. Others had noticed it. The old man on the beach. Jill at the diner. And now the quiet expert at Windward Stones. Whatever the rock had once been, someone long ago had marked it. Deliberately. For a reason.

By late afternoon, Ben was back in his room. He set the stone on the table by the window, sat on the edge of the bed, elbows on knees, shoes off. He looked at the rock, then out the window, then back again.

He reached for his journal and opened to a blank page. He paused, then wrote:

It's not about the rock. It never was. It's about what it carries—and why it won't let go of me.

He stared at the words, then closed the book, exhaled, and stood.

Time to get ready.

The parking lot outside Chinook Winds was already alive with headlights and quiet conversation. The sun had dropped below the horizon, leaving a soft, bruised sky behind it. Ben made his way through the crowd and stepped inside.

It felt like old times—the subtle excitement, the tuning of instruments on stage, the laughter, and the conversation flowing. He spotted Josh near the front, adjusting a mic stand with the same casual posture Ben remembered from decades ago.

Then, near the side of the room, he saw her.

Claire.

She stood talking with someone near the end of a row, but when she caught his eye, she smiled. Easy. Familiar.

He made his way over. "Wasn't sure I'd find you."

She laughed. "You found me."

They stood side by side as the lights dimmed and the show began. The music washed over them—melodic, weathered, full of memory.

Between songs, Claire leaned closer. "So…you really used to gig with him?"

Ben nodded. "A few shows. Back when I thought the road would save me."

She tilted her head. "And now?"

He smiled. "Now I trade stocks in the mornings and try to write in the afternoons."

Her eyebrows lifted. "You write?"

"Trying to."

"I worked in publishing," she said. "Editing. Seabrook House."

Ben blinked. "Seabrook? That's Mark Elliott's company."

"You know Mark?"

"We're friends," Ben said. "Met years ago at one of my gigs. We've stayed in touch—talk fairly often, actually."

Claire smiled. "I used to work with his wife Natalie—in the editing department."

Ben laughed quietly. "Small world keeps getting smaller."

He hesitated, then added, "Once I get the new book flowing, I'd love for you to take a look."

"I'd like that," Claire said.

They shared a look. Not loaded. Just open.

After the show, Ben told Claire he'd love to introduce her to Josh. They headed backstage, where Ben gave his name to the security staff. A few minutes later, they were waved through.

Josh grinned when he saw him. "Ben Thomas. Man, you still alive?"

"Mostly," Ben said. "Josh, this is Claire."

They talked for a while—catching up, trading old laughs. Josh mentioned he had a couple days off and would be staying local. "Let's grab lunch or something."

"I'd like that," Ben said.

Eventually, he turned to Claire. "Let me walk you to your car?"

She nodded. "Sure."

The air had turned crisp. They walked quietly at first, a calm between them that didn't need words—just the rhythm of footsteps and night. For the first time in a while, Ben didn't think about the rock or the questions that usually took up too much space in his mind. He thought about her. Her voice. Her eyes. The way she made the world feel a little more open.

At the lot, Claire stopped. "That's my car there."

Ben laughed. "No kidding. I'm three spots down."

She looked at the Corvette. "That yours?"

"Yep. Z06. It's got power to spare, but I enjoy the rumble."

Claire smiled. "Beautiful. I've always wanted to ride in one."

Ben grinned. "Well, looks like I'll be in town a little longer. Maybe you'll get your chance."

She tilted her head, smiled, and with a wink said, "That sounds like fun."

Ben watched her pull away, then stood in the dark for a moment longer, the hum of the engine fading. A breeze moved through the lot—cold, but clean. He looked up at the stars. For once, the ache wasn't what he felt pressing on his chest.

It was something else.

Something beginning.

CHAPTER 10

Mornings Like This

Ben stepped out onto the deck with a mug of coffee in hand, the ceramic warm between his fingers. The ocean spread before him in soft hues of silver and gray, the morning sky still deciding what it wanted to be. The tide had pulled back during the night, leaving a fresh canvas of wet sand below, smooth and glistening in the angled light. He took a long breath—not to inhale anything specific, but to feel the act of breathing. The salt, the silence, the stillness. All of it felt earned.

He leaned against the railing, watching a couple meander along the beach, barefoot and quiet, moving slowly as though they knew the moment was more important than the destination. Farther down, a kid ran with a dog, laughter rolling over the sand like it had no weight at all.

The sliding door next to his opened.

Claire stepped out onto her own deck, a loose cardigan wrapped around her shoulders, steam rising from the mug she carried. He noticed a softness to her now, like the night had quieted something in her. She smiled when their eyes met—nothing forced, just recognition.

"Morning," she said.

"Morning," Ben replied. "Pretty perfect out here."

She turned her gaze toward the waves. "Ever since I moved here, this coast has felt like home. Doesn't matter how many times I come—it never gets old. Always feels new somehow."

Ben nodded. "It's like it knows how to be constant without being the same."

She smiled again, and for a few moments, they stood in shared silence. The kind that wasn't awkward or waiting. Just…real.

He sipped his coffee, then glanced over. "I passed a little café yesterday. Old place with a sagging porch and flower boxes that looked half-forgotten. Couldn't tell if it was charming or sketchy, but it caught my eye."

Claire looked over, intrigued. "That sounds promising."

"I was thinking of trying it today. Would you want to come? Just lunch. My treat."

She hesitated long enough to feel sincere. "That sounds nice."

Ben nodded. "Great. I'll swing by your door around noon."

"I'll be ready," she said, then stepped back inside, leaving a faint trace of peppermint and something unplaceable in the air behind her.

Ben lingered on the deck for another minute, letting the moment settle. Something about her energy was calm but alive. And something about the way she didn't press or posture made space for his own unsettled parts.

Back inside, he set his mug down on the small desk and opened his laptop. A folder labeled "New Book" blinked back at him from the screen, like a dare. He clicked into it.

The files were sparse—just a few Word docs filled with scattered thoughts, sentences without endings, questions without answers. One was titled *Silent Challenges*. Another, *The Past of Nowhere*. A third simply read *The Weight of Life*.

He opened a blank document and stared at it for a while, the cursor pulsing like a steady breath.

Writing used to come easier—or at least more predictably. He'd written a few nonfiction books over the years—personal reflections, lived experience, essays stitched together with hope and a need to make sense of things. They didn't sell, not really. Maybe a hundred copies combined. He remembered checking the sales numbers in the early days, then pretending not to care. But the truth was, those books weren't failures. They were markers. Ways of saying *I existed. I tried.*

Now, though, something deeper was stirring.

He wasn't chasing a platform. He wasn't even sure he wanted readers. What he wanted—what he needed—was to be obedient. To whatever it was that had started pressing on his soul again. The Lord, maybe. A whisper, a wound, a presence he couldn't name but couldn't ignore.

That rock.

It carried something. A feeling that stayed with him, even in sleep.

He didn't want to write about a rock. That was ridiculous. There wasn't a story in that. And yet...he couldn't shake the sense that maybe the rock wasn't the story. Maybe it was the doorway—to something deeper. Maybe what he was really searching for was the key. The one that unlocked the mystery of *why* this thing refused to let go.

He leaned back in his chair, his fingers hovering over the keyboard, unmoving. His thoughts began to drift—not toward what lay ahead, but toward what had already been. A different time in life. A different version of himself.

He was twenty-seven, maybe twenty-eight. Newly married. Still running on caffeine and ambition and the thin hope that something bigger was waiting for him, just beyond the edge of his current life. That was the year he got the call—Johnny Cash's booking agent. They needed an extra hand at a concert just outside Portland, Oregon. Nothing glamorous. Set up. Tear down. Stay out of the way.

He remembered pulling into the venue lot early, trying to look older than he was. The tour bus was already parked out back—black and still, the letters *JC* stenciled near the rear like it carried something sacred.

And then she appeared.

June Carter Cash.

Barefoot on the gravel, coffee in one hand, clipboard in the other.

She spotted him immediately, smiled like they'd known each other for years.

"You the one they sent from down the road?" she asked.

He nodded, caught off guard. "Yes, ma'am. Just here to help with setup."

"Well," she said, "don't go running off after. I want you to grab some lunch with us backstage. You look like a boy who's been living on nerves and vending machine peanuts."

He laughed—surprised at himself, surprised at her. This was June Carter Cash, and she'd just invited him to lunch.

So he stayed.

Lunch was served on folding tables and paper plates. Johnny sat quietly in the corner, eating slow, reading something handwritten. June carried the conversation with her usual blend of sass and soul.

She asked about his life. Ben told her he played piano—not for a living, just on the side. Said he'd always dreamed of doing more, but most days, he was just trying to keep the dream from slipping away.

June leaned in, her voice lowering. "Honey, it's not all rainbows and fairy tales. Johnny and I love what we do, but there's a lot more to this life than what the crowd sees."

Then she smiled—tired, knowing. "You've got something soft in your voice. Don't lose that. Softness echoes longer than shouting ever will."

And just like that—his phone buzzed.

The motel room. The Oregon coast. Present day.

A text from Eric:

Hey, Dad, just checking in. Haven't heard from you in a few days. Fishing's been good—caught one of the biggest salmon I've ever landed.

Ben smiled. The memory still close. That was Eric. Brief. Direct. But always steady. Always there.

He typed back:

Send me a pic. I'm good—been traveling along the coast. Having a good time. Love you.

He set the phone down and glanced at the clock. 11:37. Time to freshen up, change, maybe put on a shirt that didn't look slept in.

He stood slowly, something in him feeling slightly— though unmistakably—lighter. Not in a dramatic way. Not like a man reborn. Just…more open. More aware.

A woman. A walk. A rock. A line of words waiting to be written.

Sometimes it wasn't the answers that pulled you forward. Sometimes it was the questions that refused to leave you alone.

CHAPTER 11

The Way It Starts

Ben knocked softly on Claire's door just before noon, already sensing she was nearby. Sure enough, it opened almost instantly. She was there—hair pulled back, a light jacket on, that same quiet energy she carried so effortlessly. But her smile caught him off guard.

It didn't just register—it landed. Not loud or electric. Just warm. Familiar. Like a favorite pair of worn jeans you'd forgotten still fit.

"Ready?" he asked.

She nodded. "Let's go."

They walked without hurry—the kind of pace that doesn't rush to fill silence—as they made their way toward the parking lot. The air was crisp, layered with salt and mist, and the sidewalk curved gently between beach cottages and wind-bent evergreens. The ocean was nearby—always nearby—just beyond the dunes, breathing steadily in and out.

Claire glanced over. "So…this café of yours—should I be worried?"

Ben grinned. "Absolutely. The porch is sagging, and the paint's a decade past saving. Which usually means the food's excellent."

Claire laughed. "I like your logic."

She tilted her head. "Hey… any chance we're taking the Vette?"

Ben's grin widened. "Of course. I wouldn't make you walk when we've got that baby sitting out front."

Claire lit up. "Good! I was hoping you'd say that."

She slid into the passenger seat with a casual thrill, her hand brushing the leather as she settled in. When Ben turned the key, the engine rumbled to life—low, deep, tuned like it had something to say.

Claire let out a breathy laugh. "Oh, wow! That's not just a car. That's a voice."

Ben laughed. "Exactly. It speaks my language."

The drive was short. They didn't say much—didn't need to. The car did the talking, humming low and steady through the curves of the coastal road. Claire sat back, one hand resting lightly on the door, a quiet grin on her face.

They arrived within minutes.

The café looked exactly as Ben remembered—weathered siding, a hand-painted sign, and mismatched chairs leaning against a porch that had seen better decades. Garlic and butter drifted through the air like an open invitation.

Inside, they were seated near the front window, just behind a pane of glass clouded slightly by salt and sea air. From their table, they could see the town breathing—families with strollers, older couples linked at the elbow, teenagers laughing in clusters that moved like wind.

Claire unfolded her napkin slowly. "So," she asked, glancing up, "where's home these days?"

"Redmond," Ben said. "Mostly grew up there. Left for a while. Came back a few years ago. The roots never really let go."

Her eyes widened. "You're kidding. I live in Bend."

Ben looked up, surprised. "Seriously?"

"Yeah," she said. "Moved there from Chicago about twelve years ago. It felt small at first, but it grew on me."

Ben shook his head, grinning. "That's wild. We've basically been neighbors all this time."

Claire laughed. "And we meet here—on the coast, of all places."

He raised his glass slightly. "Some stories need a few miles before they start."

The words lingered longer than expected.

She studied him. "How old are you, if you don't mind?"

"Sixty-five."

She nodded. "Fifty-eight."

He smiled. "You wear it well."

Claire laughed. "I'll take that."

Their waitress came by to take their order. Chowder for both, warm bread, and a side of fries. As she walked away, Claire leaned in a little.

"You mentioned writing. Tell me more about that."

Ben nodded. "I've written a few nonfiction books—nothing major. Personal reflections, really. Journals turned essays. They didn't sell, but that wasn't the point."

She tilted her head. "Then what was?"

He looked down for a moment, then out the window.

"I think I just needed to know I could do it. That I had something to say. These days...I'm trying again. But it's fiction now...or something close to it. Somehow, it feels more honest that way."

Claire nodded. "I get that."

"I've been journaling for over twenty years," he added. "Probably written more words than I could count. It used to feel like therapy. Now it feels like searching."

"What are you searching for?"

He shrugged. "Truth. Purpose. A reason to still be doing this. My kids are grown. My failed marriage is behind me. I trade stocks to pass time. But I keep coming back to this idea that maybe...just maybe I still have something worth putting into words."

Claire smiled gently. "I hope you do. I think you do."

A stillness settled between them. Not awkward. Just real.

Then the food came, and the conversation drifted to lighter topics—favorite books, weird movies, desserts they still remembered years later. Time thinned the way it does when things feel easy.

They had just started on their chowder when the waitress returned. "How's everything tasting for the lovely couple?"

Ben and Claire exchanged a look.

Claire laughed. "We're not a couple."

Ben chuckled. "Just met, actually."

The waitress winked. "Sure. That's how it starts."

They smiled, letting the moment pass. They didn't correct her again.

After lunch, they wandered through a few nearby shops—wood carvings, seashells, hand-poured candles, odd trinkets no one needed but everyone picked up. At one point, Claire paused at a rack of stone necklaces, her fingers brushing a small pendant.

She tilted her head. "That rock you found… I keep thinking about it."

Ben stepped beside her.

She looked over. "You said it's called Solari?"

He nodded. "That's what the old man at the shop called it."

Claire nodded slowly. "It's like it holds something. Like it remembers."

Ben met her eyes. "That's why I haven't put it away. I think there's a story in there. Or at least a question worth chasing."

She smiled. "If so, I hope you find the answers."

Just then, Ben's phone buzzed.

A text from Josh: *Hey, I'm eating at the casino tonight. Free meal. Come join me. Bring Claire too if she's up for it—she looks like a good one.*

Ben looked at her. "Josh is grabbing dinner at the casino. Invited us to join."

Claire didn't hesitate. "Yeah? That could be fun."

"You're up for it?"

She smiled. "Sure."

Ben typed a quick reply—*We're in. See you there, say 6 p.m.*—and slipped the phone back into his pocket.

CHAPTER 12

More Than a Story

Ben stayed seated, the door still shut, the hush of the ocean pressing through the windowpane. He breathed slowly—not in search of answers but waiting. Listening for God to speak.

There was only silence. Only the slow, steady rhythm of the sea.

He stood, glanced in the mirror with half a shrug, grabbed his jacket and keys, and stepped outside.

Claire was already there, leaning casually on the rail between their motel doors. A light denim jacket framed her silhouette, and her smile—soft, familiar—met him before he even said a word.

"Hey, stranger," she said.

He smiled, "You ready?"

She nodded. "Let's go."

They walked together to the car, the rhythm between them unspoken but easy. She slid into the passenger seat of the Vette like it was second nature—comfortable, settled. Ben climbed in, started the engine. The low hum of the motor filled the silence like a soundtrack waiting for its next scene.

He glanced over. "Still on board?"

Claire smirked. "Ready if you are."

They pulled onto the coast road just as the sun dipped toward the horizon, casting long strokes of gold and rose across the water. The Vette rumbled as they cruised north through the salty air, past driftwood cottages and shuttered beach shops, until the glowing lights of Chinook Winds Casino came into view.

By the time they parked, the sky had settled into deep amber, the last stretch of light painting the ocean in soft streaks of bronze and blue.

Inside, the casino carried its usual hum—slot machines chiming in the distance, low murmurs of conversation, the occasional clink of glass against glass. But past the noise and glow, the restaurant offered a quieter corner of calm.

Josh stood near the hostess stand, hands in his pockets, easy grin already in place. "Well, look who finally made it," he said.

Ben shook his head. "We're exactly on time."

Josh winked at Claire. "He always says that."

They followed him in. The table was by the window— ocean view, if the light had held a little longer. A plate of beer-battered mushrooms sat in the middle like a shared understanding, and the scent of grilled onions drifted in from the kitchen.

As they settled in, Josh raised his glass. "So, Claire—has Ben told you about his run-ins with Johnny Cash and June Carter?"

Ben shot him a look. "Shhh. Not yet."

Claire raised her brows, hand touching his arm. "My, my, Ben…you've been holding out on me."

He chuckled. "It was a long time ago. Impactful, sure. But maybe a bit much for just getting to know you."

Josh leaned back. "Trust me—you'll want to hear them. Nobody tells a story like this guy."

Claire smiled, eyes warm. "I'm intrigued. I hope I get to hear them someday."

They ate and talked—easy conversation, light and layered. Theirs was the kind of night that didn't feel like it had to prove anything.

After dinner, Ben and Claire said their goodbyes to Josh and drove toward the overlook. The Corvette purred beneath them until he shut it off. Silence settled, soft and full. Moonlight danced across the waves. The windows stayed down. The air was clean.

Ben reached to turn on the radio. Their hands brushed—quick, light—but enough to spark something between them. Neither said anything. They didn't need to.

She looked out at the water. "So…what now?"

He exhaled. "I came to Ilwaco just to get away. No real plan. I guess I was searching for something. Not even sure what. I've always come to the coast to listen—to pray. It's where I feel closest to God."

Claire nodded, eyes still on the ocean.

Ben continued, "Then I found that rock...or maybe it found me. And that scar—it felt like more than just a mark. Then I started searching for answers about the rock. And honestly, it feels like it pulled me here—to Lincoln City. And then I met you. A lot of life in just a few short days."

"I'm heading back tomorrow," she said softly. "My daughter Monica's flying in from Chicago on Friday."

Ben turned. "You have a daughter?"

"Mm-hmm. Monica. Thirty-three. Brilliant. Beautiful. She's a surgeon at Northwestern—top of her class, now one of their top staff. Brown hair, blue eyes, perfect smile. She's got a boyfriend, but it's not too serious. She's been laser-focused on her career."

Ben smiled. "Sounds like someone you're proud of."

"Very."

He paused. "Is she your only child?"

Claire nodded. "She is."

Ben leaned back. "I've got two—Melody and Eric. Melody's thirty-four. Lives in Portland. Freelance photographer. Bit of a firecracker. She's married with two kids—six and nine. My grandkids."

Claire smiled. "She sounds like fun. Kind of wild we both have daughters about the same age."

"Oh, she lights up a room. Big heart. Talks fast—like me."

Claire tilted her head. "And your son?"

"Eric's thirty-one. Quiet. Steady. Hard worker. Lives down in Coos Bay. Loves to fish and hunt. If you dropped him in the woods for two weeks, he'd be fine. Good-looking kid—takes after his dad."

Claire nudged him. "I'll bet he does."

The moment lingered. A kind of peace settled in the air between them.

Claire looked at him. "I should probably turn in soon. I've got a drive ahead of me in the morning."

"Yeah," Ben said. "I probably have a day or two left here. Funny—I didn't even plan to stay."

He looked at her. "Can I just say...this has been nice? The whole thing. I came to the coast like always—asking questions, praying, not expecting much. Then I found that rock. Then I met you."

"Life's funny like that," Claire said. "But I'm glad."

"I'd like to stay in touch," Ben said.

"I'd like that too." She handed him her phone. "Put your number in."

He tapped it in and handed it back with a small smile.

They sat in stillness for another quiet minute. Then he started the engine—the Vette giving its usual low rumble.

They pulled out slowly, the conversation giving way to a silence that didn't need filling.

At the motel, he walked her to her door. She turned, leaned in, and kissed him gently on the cheek.

"Thanks for a beautiful couple of days," she said. "I hope you start that book. I hope you figure out what the rock really means."

Ben nodded. "So do I."

She stepped inside, leaving a quiet smile behind her.

Ben stood there for a moment, hands in his pockets, eyes on the dim walkway ahead. The air was cool. Still. The kind of stillness that doesn't beg for answers—only presence.

Back in his room, he moved slower than usual. Not tired. Just full. The way you feel after a moment that meant more than it let on.

He sat on the edge of the bed, pulled out his phone, and sent a quick text to Melody:

Just checking in. I love you. Sleep well.

Then he set the phone aside and opened his journal. He stared at the page for a while before writing:

God... what is all this? Am I dreaming—or is this what waking up finally feels like?

He paused, then added:

I'm not looking for signs anymore. Just enough light to take one more step.

He closed the journal and set it on the nightstand.

Then he lay back on the bed, eyes on the ceiling, breath steady, the hum of the ocean in the distance.

Years had passed since he felt this kind of ache—the good kind that meant he was alive again.

Sleep came slowly. But not empty.

Not this time.

CHAPTER 13

A Stranger Remembered

The morning came with a kind of reluctance—soft light through a salted curtain, the distant hush of waves folding in and out. Ben moved slowly. Not from fatigue, but from the ache that goodbyes often leave behind—even when they're not permanent.

Claire stood outside her room, suitcase at her feet, phone in hand. She looked up as he stepped out, that same calm smile waiting for him.

"Well," she said gently, "this is where I head east."

"Bend," he nodded.

"Yep. Beautiful Bend," she said with a grin.

They shared a quiet moment, the space between them holding more than words could carry. Ben stepped forward and pulled her into a hug. It lingered—not too long, not too short. Just enough for something to almost happen.

She pulled back slightly, eyes still on his, and for a breath they hovered—on the edge of something unnamed.

But the moment passed.

"Drive safe," he said. "Enjoy your time with Monica."

"Thanks," she said. "I hope you figure out what the rock—Solari—is trying to say."

"I'm working on it."

She started to turn, then looked back. "Let's talk once we're both home?"

He nodded. "I'd like that."

And then she was gone.

Ben lingered by the railing after she drove off, the cool morning air brushing his face, the ocean stretching wide and unapologetic behind him. He slipped the rock into his pocket and made his way down to the beach.

The coast was alive with people that afternoon. Kids ran barefoot in the wet sand, couples walked hand in hand, kites sliced across the sky. Everyone seemed to be moving—forward, together, fully present. Ben felt like he was floating through it all, just a few steps behind the rhythm of the world.

He walked without destination, enjoying the sound of the surf and the slow give of sand beneath his feet. His thoughts drifted, wide and heavy, with that same question trailing him like fog:

What now?

A boy caught his eye—maybe seven or eight—sprinting through the shallows, shouting with joy as he held up a smooth gray stone. He ran to a man—his father, probably— who bent to examine it like treasure.

They laughed. No rush. No fear. Just life.

Ben smiled, then felt something catch in his throat. He turned toward the horizon.

Where did life go? What was this week? A break in the current—or the start of something I don't yet have a name for?

His heel brushed something in the sand. He looked down.

A sand dollar—whole, perfect, like it had been waiting for him.

He crouched, picked it up, and turned it gently in his hand. The detail stunned him. So fragile. So deliberate.

God, You made this. You made the waves, the wind, that little boy...and the rock in my pocket. You made Claire. You made me. I'm not asking for signs. I'm asking for a story. A voice. Something alive in me again.

He stood slowly, still holding the sand dollar, when a voice behind him called out.

"Ben? Ben Thomas?"

He turned. A woman stood there—early fifties, maybe a little older—her eyes bright with recognition.

"I knew it," she said. "I saw you play at the Seabird Theater in Bandon—what, fifteen years ago? You made that old piano sing like it had a soul."

Ben chuckled, caught off guard. "That was a long time ago."

"You told a story that night. About Johnny and June. About how she once said all she wanted was to walk through a grocery store holding Johnny's hand—just buy food like a normal couple. But they couldn't go anywhere without being stopped for a picture or an autograph. She said, 'Most people have freedoms we're no longer allowed. Don't ever take that for granted.'"

Ben blinked. "You remember that?"

She smiled. "I never forgot it. Made me appreciate my quiet life a little more. Privacy. Simplicity. You gave me that."

He nodded, humbled. "Thank you. That means more than you know."

"What are you doing now?"

"Semi-retired," he said. "Trying to write a book. Maybe."

"Well," she said, smiling, "put that story in there. It's a good one."

He promised he'd think about it, and they said their goodbyes. She walked north. He walked south.

Later, after a simple dinner in town, Ben returned to the motel just as the sky began its slow fade. He sat on the small deck outside his room and listened to the waves—the kind of sound that doesn't demand attention but offers peace if you let it.

His phone buzzed.

Claire: *Just wanted to let you know I made it home safe. Might've thought about you more than I should have today.*

Ben smiled, then sent back a simple reply:

Ben: *Glad you made it. I'll probably head home tomorrow.*

In Bend Claire read the message and smiled—then paused. He didn't say he thought of me. She bit her lip, unsure whether she'd said too much or just enough.

Back in his room, Ben opened his laptop. The screen lit up—blank page, cursor blinking. He began to type:

Sometimes the story doesn't arrive all at once. Sometimes it's a whisper through the mist, a scar in stone, or the way a stranger remembers something you forgot you gave.

I'm not chasing meaning anymore. I'm listening for it. Maybe that's what the rock was trying to say all along.

He stared at the words.

Then slowly closed the laptop.

Outside, the waves kept speaking—slow, steady, ancient. Ben didn't answer.

He just listened.

CHAPTER 14

A Voice Returning

Ben moved slowly that morning—not out of reluctance, but reverence. There was something about the quiet rhythm of leaving a place that had mattered. He folded his clothes with care, rinsed the coffee mug, zipped the bag with a finality that wasn't heavy, just honest. Then he stepped out into the crisp morning air, letting it settle across his shoulders.

His phone vibrated as he locked the motel door behind him.

Ben— I've been thinking about our time in Lincoln City. I wasn't expecting any of it. You have a quiet way of asking questions without pushing. I appreciated that. I still don't know what the scar means—not yours, not the one on the rock—but I believe it matters. If you ever write about it, I'd like to read it. Take care driving home. And thank you. –Claire

He stood with the phone in his hand, her words stirring something gentle beneath his chest. Not fire. Not ache. Just warmth. Presence. An echo that stayed.

He didn't rush to reply. Just walked to the car, tossed the bag behind the seat, and eased behind the wheel. The engine rumbled to life with its familiar low hum. He sat for a moment before pulling out, his eyes on the road that stretched east.

He wasn't running—not this time. He was simply heading home.

The coast slipped behind him as the trees closed in along the winding road. Fog hung over the hills like a veil, and the pavement glided beneath the tires in a slow, knowing rhythm.

Ben let the quiet ride with him. No music. No news. No need to fill the air.

There was no grand epiphany. No divine download. Just the quiet sense that something inside had shifted. Not finished—just different. Calmer. More whole.

For a long time, life had felt like a tangle he couldn't unravel. He had carried pain, yes—but pain wasn't the headline anymore. He was healing. Gradually. Quietly. But truly.

Somewhere outside Philomath, he passed a stretch of fields still heavy with dew. A lone crow flew beside the road for several seconds, then veered toward the trees. Ben watched it go—not because it meant something, but because it was there. And for once, that was enough.

His house in Redmond appeared like a familiar song—same notes, heard differently now.

He parked in the drive and turned off the engine. The world exhaled around him.

He stood at the door for a moment, keys in hand. Then he stepped inside.

It smelled clean. Still. Like a space that had been waiting, but not impatiently. The light through the blinds felt softer than he remembered. Or maybe he was just seeing it more clearly.

He walked through each room like greeting an old friend—kitchen, living room, hallway. The office still held the quiet hum of machines he hadn't touched in days. His trading screens sat dark. He didn't turn them on. Not today.

He poured a cup of coffee, black and strong, and opened a few windows. The breeze moved through the house like a tide—gentle and cleansing.

At the desk, he picked up his phone and tapped out a few quick messages.

Melody – I'm home. Hope you're well. Love you.
Eric – Got home this afternoon. Thinking of you. Love you.

He hesitated. Then typed one more:

Claire – I made it home. Thank you—for your message. And for... everything, really. There's more I'd like to share, eventually. And I'd love to hear more of your story too. No rush. Oh—and I've been thinking of you too.

He sent it. No expectations. Just truth.

That evening, he sat on the edge of his bed. His laptop was open. Blank page. Cursor waiting.

He stared at the screen—not afraid, just aware. Aware of what it meant to begin.

I've spent too many years watching life instead of living it. I've worn masks I didn't even realize I put on. Smiled when I was tired. Pushed through when I should've paused. I thought strength meant staying silent. But I'm learning it means telling the truth. Not loudly. Not to prove anything. Just honestly. I don't know what this story is yet. But I know I have to write it. Not for applause. Not for closure. Just to stop hiding.

He sat back. Let the weight of it settle. Then typed a few more lines. Not polished. Not perfect. But real.

A beginning.

A voice returning.

A man not escaping his past—but finally ready to speak from it.

CHAPTER 15

The Turning Point

The text came early, just as the first light began to soften the edges of the blinds in Ben's kitchen.

Dropping Monica off at the Portland International Airport. Early flight. Should be back mid-afternoon if traffic's not awful.

Ben read it while the kettle heated, standing barefoot on the cold tile, the hem of his flannel pants brushing his ankles. He smiled slightly and thumbed a reply.

Drive safe. If you're not too wiped out, maybe dinner later?

He set the phone on the counter, spooned coffee grounds into the press, and paused. The silence in his house was different from the motels on the coast—less wild, more measured. Familiar. The kind of silence that carried routine in its bones.

He leaned against the counter, letting the kettle warm, and listened. The heater kicked on with a soft clunk, pushing warmth through the vents. Somewhere beyond the backyard, a bird—not a seagull this time—called once, sharp and echoing through the trees. The old wall clock above the pantry ticked steadily, each second falling like a drop in a bucket he hadn't noticed was filling.

It felt strange, this return to rhythm. Almost suspicious. Like life was offering him a pace he hadn't earned.

A minute later, her response lit up the screen across the counter.

That'd be nice. I'd like that.

He smiled. Not a broad grin—just something quiet and involuntary. Then he poured the water, pressed the grounds, and watched the swirl of steam rise like breath exhaled into morning.

Something about the way she said it—not effusive, not forced, just steady—settled into him like the soft strike of a single piano key in an empty room: barely there, but impossible to ignore.

The coffee tasted richer than anything he'd had on the coast. Not bitter. Not burnt. Just full-bodied and rounded, with the kind of depth that stays on the tongue. He carried it out to the deck, where the air still held a trace of chill, though the sun had begun its slow climb above the trees.

The deck boards creaked beneath him—familiar now, no longer foreign. He settled into the chair that faced east, mug in one hand, laptop balanced on his legs like a sleeping dog. The screen was already on—a blinking cursor waiting for instruction. Waiting for purpose.

He had neither.

What he had was a feeling. Not loud. Not urgent. Just persistent. Like something shifting deep below the surface—slow tectonic movement, unseeable but inevitable.

He thought about the book he'd once planned to write. The idea had come almost fully formed, months ago—a veiled retelling of his own unraveling. A story wrapped in fiction but rooted in the real pain he'd never quite named. Divorce. Disappointment. The decades he'd spent carrying guilt like something sacred.

He'd imagined a character—someone like him but not quite—walking through shame, climbing out of the wreckage of his choices. On paper, it had seemed like the perfect vessel: honest enough to carry weight, distant enough to keep him from drowning in it. He'd outlined it all, thinking structure would guide him through his own wreckage.

But the words refused to move.

Every time he sat down to begin, the voice inside him went silent. Or worse—spun in circles. And the one thing he could never solve, no matter how many drafts he sketched, was the ending. He always stalled somewhere in the middle. Like a car approaching a turn it didn't believe in.

So he'd gone to the coast, hoping salt and silence might shake something loose. Hoping the rhythm of the waves might pull him through.

But what stirred wasn't the story he went there to write.

It was something else. Something quieter. Older, maybe. Or newer. He wasn't sure.

It began with a rock. A scarred one. Half-buried in the sand, catching light like it had been waiting.

And from there—everything had shifted.

He hadn't noticed it at the time. But now, in hindsight, it was obvious: the old story—the one centered on pain— began to fade the moment he picked up that stone. The wounds didn't vanish, but they stopped demanding to be at the center of the page.

He took a slow sip of coffee, his eyes following a bird gliding through the branches. The laptop hummed lightly, waiting.

He rested his fingers on the keys. Still no outline. No title. But the weight he had carried—the need to explain himself, to bleed into the story—had been replaced by something quieter.

He began to type, not with certainty, but with peace.

The story I thought I needed to tell—the one about everything I lost, everything I broke—that story isn't mine anymore. Maybe it never was.

I was trying to shape pain into a purpose. But maybe the real purpose is in putting it down. Letting it go.

He sat back. Let the words hang in the air.

Then leaned forward again and typed:

I thought healing would come through writing about the wound. But maybe healing is what happens when you stop needing to explain it. When you stop needing to carry it alone.

His coffee had gone cold. He didn't care. He looked up at the sky, then down at the blinking cursor. A heartbeat.

He didn't know what kind of book this would become. He wasn't even sure it would be a book at all. But something in him had turned. Like a tide shifting direction—silent, but absolute.

For the first time, he wasn't writing to be understood.

He was writing because he finally understood.

Not everything.

But enough.

He still believed in truth. In story. In a strange, sacred way they could stitch a person back together. But this time, he wasn't writing to publish. He wasn't chasing anything— not approval, not redemption, not recognition.

He was just answering a call. Quiet. Persistent. Like breath.

And whatever came of it—whether the words stayed tucked away in a forgotten file or somehow became something someone might one day hold in their hands—that wasn't his to control.

That part belonged to God.

As he sat thinking about the story he was beginning to feel and shape, he wondered: *Is it even worth it? All these hours...searching for the right words. Will it even help anyone?*

Just then, his phone buzzed.

Eric: *Hey Dad, just thinking about you. I was reading a book about the choices we make—made me think of you. How you love to write. I hope you keep doing it.*

Ben smiled and typed back:

Ben: *Perfect timing. I started working on a new book a few days ago. Well, maybe it started even before that. Either way, I appreciate your words. I love you.*

It felt like God had used Eric to send a gentle nudge. Not loud, not dramatic. Just a quiet yes. Keep going. Keep searching. Keep writing.

CHAPTER 16

Not Just a Story

The text came just after five.

Home. Tired. Traffic was as bad as you'd expect. But I made it. Let me know if dinner still sounds good.

Ben thumbed a reply.

I know a quiet spot. Nothing fancy, but the view's solid, and the food doesn't lie.

Her next message arrived after a longer pause than before.

That sounds perfect. Can we make it later? I need a minute to decompress. Maybe 7:00?

Take your time, he wrote back. *I'll be there when you're ready.*

He didn't dress up. Just brushed his teeth, washed his face, changed his shirt. Then he sat on the deck with a mug of coffee in hand, watching the soft bend of light stretch across the lawn as evening settled in. The quiet didn't ask anything of him. It just held him.

By six o'clock, he felt ready—not to perform, not to charm, just to be present.

The drive was quick. Almost too easy. Like heading to a concert he'd waited months to see, only to realize it was already there. The roads were familiar, but they looked different somehow—like time had softened their edges while he wasn't paying attention.

He waited outside the small restaurant tucked behind a forgotten bookstore. No big sign. Just a weathered door and soft jazz bleeding from the seams. He'd picked the place because it didn't try to impress—just warm food, a clear view, and enough quiet for a real conversation.

Claire arrived right on time.

She looked relaxed—tired, maybe, but soft around the edges. A sweater over a plain top, jeans, flats. No makeup. No pretense. Just herself. That was enough.

They started light—her daughter's nerves about work, Ben's frustration with market swings and weak coffee. They laughed about Portland drivers and restaurant menus that tried too hard. But somewhere between the salad and the main course, the mood shifted.

"You mentioned once," Claire said, setting her fork down, "that you worked with Johnny Cash. You were serious, right?"

Ben smiled—not wide, but real. "Yeah. Though it's not as glamorous as it sounds."

"Tell me."

He leaned back. "It started by accident. A friend of mine traveled as a tech on their crew. One night they were short a guy—needed someone who could wire a few things, tune a guitar, keep out of the way. My name came up. I got a call the next morning from Johnny's manager. Just like that, I was backstage."

Claire's eyes lit up. "That's wild."

"It wasn't regular work. Just a couple of gigs. But it got me in the room. First time was up north, a big arena show. I kept quiet. Johnny barely spoke to anyone. But June..." He smiled wider. "She had enough energy for three people."

Claire laughed softly. "I believe it."

"She made everyone feel like they belonged. Told stories while pacing in heels, a mic in one hand and hairspray in the other. It was like standing in a whirlwind. She loved the road. The people. Fame and fortune were just background noise to her. What she lived for was connection."

He paused, looking out the window.

"The second time I helped was farther south at a county fairground. They remembered me. That night felt different. Calmer. More real. Johnny stayed quiet, mostly on the bus. But June...she talked like we were old friends. Told me things I still haven't forgotten."

Claire was silent, watching him closely.

"She told me about a letter they got. A woman's little boy was dying of cancer. The mother begged them to visit the hospital—not because the boy knew who Johnny Cash was, but because she had lived through his songs. She believed, somehow, if he just sat with her son, it might bring healing."

Claire exhaled. "Did they go?"

Ben shook his head. "No. And June hated that answer. Not because she didn't care. But because she knew it wasn't Johnny the woman needed."

He looked straight at Claire.

"June said, 'She was asking the wrong JC.'"

Claire blinked.

Ben nodded. "That's what she told me. Not harsh. Just honest. She said Johnny was a man. Flawed, burdened, tired. He could sing truth, carry pain, bleed it into melody—but he wasn't Jesus. And pretending otherwise would've been a lie."

He paused. "That moment changed me. The way she said it—it was like truth carving something open."

Claire's voice came soft. "That's the story people should hear. Not the shine. The scar. The pain, yes—but maybe more than that…the truth. The kind that doesn't try to impress anyone. The kind that just stands there and says, '*This is what it cost me.*'"

Ben nodded. "That's the story I want to tell. In the book. In life. That's the one that matters."

Claire was quiet for a moment, then reached for her glass but didn't lift it.

Her voice dropped. "I have a story too."

He met her eyes, steady. "I'd like to hear it."

"I'm not ready tonight," she said. "It's not small. And I don't know where this is going—you and me. But if we're walking forward, you need to know what I carry."

Ben's hand moved across the table to gently cover hers.

"I want to know *you*," he said. "Not just the woman smiling at me tonight. All of it. The whole story."

Claire smiled—soft, tentative, grateful. "Maybe tomorrow. Maybe we walk. I tend to think clearer when I move. And I'll need air. A lot of it."

Ben smiled back. "Then we'll walk."

CHAPTER 17

The Scars We Carry

Ben brewed a fresh cup of coffee and stepped out onto the deck, the morning air still holding its cool edge. The breeze carried a softness that reminded him of the coast—quiet, expectant, like something waiting to unfold. He settled into his chair, placed the mug beside his laptop, and began to write.

He didn't have a title yet. He rarely did at the start of a new project. Titles came later—once the work had shape, breath, and a soul. Until then, he preferred to let things remain unnamed. Creation, he believed, needed freedom before it needed definition.

This story was different. It wasn't memoir. It wasn't nonfiction. It was fiction—but not a departure from truth. If anything, it felt like truth told from the inside out. The scar, the warmth, the mystery of the rock—those threads had begun to weave themselves into something larger than his own story. They were becoming symbols of something deeper, something universal. He still didn't know where it would all lead. He didn't need to. For now, he was just laying down the bones.

Claire's words from the night before echoed in his mind, lingering long after the stories he'd shared about Johnny and June: *Not the shine. The scar. The truth. The kind that says, "This is what it cost me."*

He paused, letting the words settle in his chest.

Ben had loved Jesus most of his adult life. He read Scripture, journaled regularly, and prayed often. But if he was honest, he hadn't always let himself sit with the cost of what that love meant—the suffering, the weight of it. He'd known it, believed it, but maybe not carried it close.

We go to church. We hear the sermons. We read of the crucifixion in the pages of Scripture. And then we go on with our day.

But something in him had started to shift. He couldn't explain it exactly. The story of the cross didn't feel as far away anymore. It was like the edges were drawing closer—closer than he'd let them before.

He sipped his coffee. The morning drifted by.

Just before noon, he sent Claire a text: *Hey. Just thinking of you. You still up for that walk today?*

A few minutes passed before her reply came: *As ready as I'll ever be, I suppose. Let's say around 1. The little park by the river on the east side of town—the one with the trails that skirt the bend. You know the one I mean?*

I do, Ben replied. *Been there often. Peaceful place. See you at 1.*

He closed his laptop, took a breath, and whispered a simple prayer. He wasn't sure what to say. He didn't even know exactly what to ask for—just that the Lord would be present. That whatever Claire needed to release, she would find the grace to say it and peace on the other side.

At 1:03, they met in the gravel parking lot near the trailhead. Claire looked different—quieter somehow, as if carrying something she hadn't yet named aloud. Her smile was soft, but her eyes were uncertain.

"Hey," she said. Her voice was steady, but she looked down as the word left her mouth.

Ben smiled, didn't press. "Hey."

They started walking slowly at first. No rush. No small talk. Just the sound of footsteps and the hush of trees overhead. Claire kept her hands in her jacket pockets, gazing mostly on the path ahead.

About ten minutes in, she spoke. "About twenty-three years ago," she said, "I was living in Chicago. Married. Monica was ten. My husband was a police officer. It was a Thursday. I remember because he'd left for work around nine. I'd sent Monica off to school. Just a normal morning."

She paused. Ben said nothing. Just stayed beside her, steady.

"I was in the bathroom, freshening up. I heard a sound. Something off. Not something I could explain—just a feeling that didn't sit right. I called out, 'Hello?' I don't even know why. Instinct, maybe."

She paused again. Her hands were trembling now. She reached for Ben's hand. He took it without hesitation.

"I'm sorry," she said, voice cracking. "This is going to be harder than I thought it would be."

"I'm here," Ben said gently. "Take your time."

Claire nodded, breathed in deep. "I won't go into graphic detail. I...I can't. But when I stepped out of the bathroom, he was there. A man. A stranger. I didn't know him. He grabbed me. Ripped my shirt. Put a knife to my throat. Whispered...'This will be done soon. Don't fight me, and you won't die.'"

Ben felt his stomach drop.

Claire went on, eyes focused straight ahead. "I prayed to God it wasn't real. But it was. I thought about my husband. About Monica. I wondered if I'd see them again. He pulled me into the bedroom and held me there. He...he raped me."

Ben squeezed her hand. She didn't let go.

"It was brutal," she said quietly. "It wasn't just what he did. It was what he took. I wasn't the same after. I don't think I ever will be."

They walked a few more steps before she continued.

"After that, I fell apart. I blamed myself in ways I didn't even realize. I kept asking, 'Why me?' I'd loved the Lord since I was a little girl. I'd tried to live right. But I felt like I'd been chosen for something horrific, and I couldn't understand why."

She swallowed. "Over the next two years, I disappeared. Not physically, but emotionally. My husband couldn't bear it. I shut him out. I couldn't stand being touched. I tried, I really did, but I couldn't pretend to be whole. Eventually, he left. He met someone else. They're married now. He's a good man. Lives in Houston. He and Monica still talk. But I was…unlovable."

Ben stopped walking. Claire did too.

"I'm so sorry," he said. "You are not unlovable. Not even close."

She looked at him. Eyes full of tears, but she smiled—just barely.

"About a year after the assault, they caught the man for other crimes. He was sentenced to fifty-three years. Still in prison today." She paused. "But for a long time, I lived in a prison of my own. No bars. Just fear. And shame."

Ben reached into his pocket and pulled out the scarred rock—an old habit by now. Claire looked at it, surprised.

He held it out.

She touched the scar with her thumb.

"That," she said, "is what I carry."

Ben nodded.

"A man chose to harm me. To carve his shame into my life. He gave me a scar I never asked for—one I didn't deserve. But I live with it. Not just the memory—but the mark."

She took a breath.

"But the event itself? That's over. What's left is just the scar. And what we choose to do with it...that's where the story is."

Ben didn't speak. He didn't need to.

Claire went on. "I moved here twelve years ago. It wasn't an escape. It was a beginning. I felt something shift—a healing I can't explain. Not that everything got easier overnight. But I learned to breathe again. To forgive."

She looked down at the rock again. "His name was Carl. The man who scarred me for life—Carl. Even saying it still stings." Her voice caught, but she didn't pull away. "But I forgave him. Not because he asked—he never did. But because I had to. I had Monica. I had a life still worth living. And I couldn't let that man own another inch of it."

Ben's voice came quiet. "Claire, I had no idea. You seem so...whole."

"I'm not," she said. "Not completely. But I'm alive. I'm breathing. I'm moving forward. That counts for something."

He nodded. "It counts for everything."

She smiled through her tears. "I don't know why I felt safe enough to tell you. I can't explain these last few weeks—the beach, the timing, you. But I think God brought us together. Maybe just to share our stories. Maybe to remind each other that life doesn't always give us answers. Some parts leave a mark, yes—but those marks, those scars, they don't have to define the rest of the story. Not unless we let them."

Ben looked out over the trail, the light shifting through the trees. "Maybe that's what the book needs to be about. Not just my past. Not just pain. But the choice to keep breathing. To walk forward."

Claire nodded. "Maybe someone needs to hear that story. Maybe someone like me."

Ben took her hand again. "Thank you for trusting me."

Claire nodded, eyes still glistening.

"I don't know what this is between us," she said quietly. "But I know it's real."

Ben held her gaze. "I won't forget your story. Or your strength."

They stood there a moment longer—two people bound not by romance or convenience, but by something older and deeper.

Grace. Shared pain. And the long road toward healing.

CHAPTER 18

Chapters Without Endings

Ben sat in his home office, coffee cooling beside him, laptop open in front of him. The room was quiet, filled with morning light that slanted through the blinds and stretched across the floor in soft lines. Outside, the air had a crispness to it—clear, still, the kind that sharpened your focus without pushing you inside.

It had been two days since the walk with Claire—since she trusted him with a truth that didn't alter how he saw her but deepened his understanding of her strength. The kind that speaks gently, softened by sorrow, not hardened by it.

He hadn't written much the day after. Just a few lines. But something inside had shifted. Not forced. Not loud. Just... ready.

Now, the words came differently—faster, but without force. They didn't surge, but they didn't stall either. He wasn't chasing pain anymore. He was writing from a different place—still shaped by what he'd walked through but no longer defined by it. The story had stopped being about struggle and started being about survival. About how the scar meant the bleeding had stopped.

He typed:

We carry pain, but we also carry breath. The mark proves we lived through it. The real miracle isn't in the healing—it's in the choosing to live while still marked.

Ben sat back and reread the line. It was the kind of sentence that didn't need polishing. It just needed to be true.

The book was taking shape. Not all at once, but piece by piece. Four chapters now. Maybe more soon. He didn't have an ending, and he wasn't sure he wanted one yet. Life didn't always hand you answers in a neat little package tied off with resolution. Sometimes it just asks you to keep going.

He reached for his phone and sent Claire a short text:

You were right. The truth is the story. I've written four chapters—none of them perfect, but they're honest.

Her reply came not long after:

I'd love to read them.

Later that afternoon, Ben called Eric.

His son picked up on the second ring. "Hey, Dad. Everything okay?"

"Yeah, just checking in. Been thinking about you."

Eric sounded surprised, but not unpleasantly. "You're not calling about the house or money or anything?"

Ben laughed. "Nope. Just wanted to hear your voice."

They talked about work. About fishing. About anything and nothing at all. It was good. Easy.

"I'm proud of you, you know," Ben said at the end. "Even if I don't always say it."

Eric was quiet for a heartbeat. "Thanks, Dad. That means a lot."

They hung up, and Ben sat with that. Not regret. Just a soft ache. The kind that comes with time lost and time reclaimed.

That evening, Melody texted him a photo of the sunset from her apartment balcony.

This made me think of you. You'd say the clouds looked like an old piano ballad.

Ben chuckled and wrote back:

They do. Something slow. Minor key. Lots of unresolved chords.

She replied instantly:

That's life, huh? One big unresolved chord.

He stared at her words. Then saved the text. *Maybe it will make it into the book.*

By the weekend, he had seven chapters—some more polished than others. He didn't force them. He just showed up each morning and let the words rise. He stopped worrying about structure. He let the story breathe.

On Sunday afternoon, he met Claire at the same café from their first dinner. She wore a soft blue sweater and a long scarf knotted loosely around her neck. Her eyes were calmer now, less guarded.

They talked about Monica, about Melody and Eric, about how everything outside felt like it was slowly waking up again. Then, gently, she asked, "When can I read some of it—the book? Or...sorry, the pages that might become a book?"

He hesitated, but only for a moment. "Soon," he said.

"I'd like that."

"I would too," he said. "It's not perfect. It's probably not even clear yet. But I think the story's starting to trust me."

She smiled. "Then I'll read it with the same trust."

Excerpt from Ben's book:

It's not about avoiding pain. That's not the promise. The promise is that even in pain, we are not alone. That even in what nearly breaks us, there's breath. And if there's breath, there's still story. Not every chapter needs to resolve. Some just need to be written.

They finished their coffee slowly. No big conversation. No push. Just presence.

Ben walked her to her car. They didn't hug, didn't make promises. But something had been exchanged—a quiet kind of companionship that didn't need explaining.

He went home that night and opened the laptop again. He didn't write. He just stared at the blinking cursor, felt the silence around it.

He still didn't know how the story would end. But for the first time, that didn't scare him.

Because he was writing from breath now—not for the outcome. But for the honesty of the page.

CHAPTER 19

The Feeling's Mutual

Ben was home, still writing—deep into a story about healing, hope, love, forgiveness, and strength. The ending remained unclear, but the pages were beginning to take shape.

Over the next two days, he kept sorting through his thoughts. The words flowed steadily, and he let them. He wrote about scars and surrender, about the quiet places where grief and grace overlap. He thought about Claire. About the beach. About how life could be confusing and complex, yet strangely simple at the same time. He wasn't sure that even made sense—but then again, when had life ever truly made sense in a way you could fully figure it out?

On the third evening, he invited Claire over for dinner.

The meal was simple but meaningful. Ben had made a dish he remembered from years back. Claire was impressed.

She said it tasted like a slice of heaven. She brought dessert—cheesecake—and they lingered at the table, savoring the food, the quiet, and the comfort of each other's presence.

After the plates were cleared, Ben asked, "Well…are you ready to read what I have?"

She nodded and stood up, rinsing a few dishes in the sink. She opened a cabinet, unsure where he kept towels and soap—small domestic uncertainties that made her smile.

She made her way to the couch. Ben went to his office and returned with the laptop. He handed it to her and let it rest across her lap.

"I'll be in my office," he said gently. "Doing some chart work, maybe prepping for tomorrow's trades. Take your time. Enjoy." He smiled softly, then disappeared down the hall.

Claire began to read.

The house grew quiet. Thirty minutes passed, maybe more. Ben heard nothing—no comments, no questions. Just stillness. He hoped the words were speaking to her, that maybe, even in reading, she was finding a kind of healing—the way he had, almost without realizing it, simply by writing.

Eventually, she appeared at his office door.

"Do you have a minute?" she asked, her voice soft, her eyes a little unsteady.

"Sure," he said, rising from his chair.

She didn't say anything at first. She just hugged him—tight. Not like their earlier embraces. This one carried meaning. Depth.

She took his hand and led him quietly back to the living room. They sat on the couch in silence.

Then she spoke, voice cracking slightly. "Ben, you have a gift. I worked in editing—with Mark's wife, Natalie, like I told you. I've read a lot of fiction in my life, but this…I'm not even sure how to put it into words. It's like the rock you found. I can't explain what I feel exactly, but somehow your words reached something inside me I didn't even know was there."

Ben felt pride, relief, something swelling in his chest—but he knew this wasn't about him. He wasn't the story. He wasn't writing for his own glory.

Time seemed to stretch. Only a few seconds passed, but something had shifted.

"Thank you," he said. His eyes brimmed. He tried to hold it together, but a single tear escaped and landed on her hand.

They looked at each other. And then, a kiss—not scripted, not expected. Just a moment. Nothing rushed. Nothing dramatic. But full of meaning. Years of pain, from both, wrapped into those few seconds.

When it passed, they smiled, took a breath, and returned to reality. Neither of them spoke of who kissed whom—it didn't matter. It was mutual. It was wanted. That was enough.

"That was nice," Ben said.

She smiled. "I agree."

One more soft kiss followed—an unspoken yes.

Claire laughed. "Is it hot in here?"

Ben chuckled. The tension broke, just enough.

He got up and pulled some lemonade from the fridge. He handed her a glass, and together they stepped out onto the deck.

The evening was settling in. They didn't know where this would go. But something inside both had settled. For now, it was enough.

Claire sipped her drink, then looked out toward the trees. "I know you're just writing—still shaping it. And I know you're unsure about the ending or even if this will ever become a finished manuscript. But…I think Mark and Natalie need to see this."

Ben leaned back. "I don't know if I'm ready to jump that far ahead. I'm finding healing in writing this book like nothing I've ever experienced. There's been more peace in the past few weeks than I've felt in years. And your story really helped me keep going. Helped me find the thread I didn't even know I was looking for."

He paused. "I'm still not sure if this is just for me, or maybe for us, or if it's meant for anyone else at all. But I won't rule it out. Maybe…someday."

Claire nodded. "Mark would have a pretty good sense if it has potential."

Ben pulled back slightly. "But I don't want to write for money."

Claire stepped in gently. "Ben, let God work out the details—who, what, when, and where. You just keep writing. Keep pouring your heart and soul into it. It's worth pressing on. And Mark deserves the chance to see it—even if it's just to help you shape it."

Ben nodded. "Okay," he said. "I'll let you know when I'm ready."

CHAPTER 20

The Words We Carry

A few days passed, and Ben's thoughts drifted in and out. He kept thinking about Claire—the kiss, the quiet moments they'd shared, and what any of it meant. It felt like he'd lived a lifetime over the past several weeks. The days and nights had started to blur together as he lost himself in the story unfolding on his laptop. For the first time in years, maybe ever, he felt like a writer. Not someone trying to write—but a storyteller.

He and Claire had been texting now and then, nothing too serious. They hadn't talked about the kiss. She asked about the book sometimes, and he'd share small pieces—never too much, just glimpses. It was easier that way. Simpler. Like they were giving each other space without saying they needed it.

That morning, Ben had been writing since just after sunrise. The first mug of coffee had long gone cold. A second sat half-full beside him, untouched. The keys tapped steadily in the quiet of the house as he finished a paragraph, then paused—letting the sentence settle before moving on.

He heard the knock before the doorbell. Soft, almost shy. He rose, stretched, and opened the door.

Claire stood there—simple and radiant. No makeup, no presentation—just her.

"Hey," she said.

"Hey."

She stepped in, and before either of them said another word, they met in a soft kiss. Nothing forced. Nothing staged. Just a continuation of something that had already begun.

They pulled apart slowly, smiles trading places as they walked inside.

"It smells like thinking in here," Claire said.

Ben laughed. "That bad?"

"No," she said. "That good."

She followed him into the office, where his screen glowed with half-finished sentences. Four new chapters were under-way—rough, but alive.

Claire pulled up a chair beside him. "Mind if I sit in?"

"Not at all."

She leaned gently on the back of his chair, resting her hand on his shoulder. He resumed typing, and she read along quietly as the words unfolded. Occasionally, she murmured a comment—a phrasing she liked, a question about a line, an idea that gave him the nudge to keep going.

When the momentum paused, she said, "How about I make us some lunch?"

Ben nodded. "Sure. Make yourself at home. I'll show you where everything is."

They moved into the kitchen together. Ben pulled open cabinets, pointed out the essentials. Claire smiled as she took it in—his small systems, the familiar clutter of a home lived in but not polished.

Ten minutes later, she called from the dining room. "Hey, storyteller. Lunch is ready. Take a break."

He closed his laptop, brought it with him, and sat across from her at the table.

"Mind if I read a little while we eat?" she asked.

"Feel free."

She opened the laptop and started reading while they shared a simple meal—grilled sandwiches, salad, and apple slices on the side. A few minutes in, she chuckled softly.

Ben looked up. "What?"

She smiled and read aloud: "Maybe it's not about finding peace before you move forward. Maybe it's in the moving forward that peace finds you."

"Ben," she said, eyes still on the screen, "that's not just good writing. That's truth."

He didn't answer. Just kept eating, a quiet smile forming as he watched her take it in.

After lunch, she closed the laptop gently.

"I needed that," she said.

Ben smiled.

He offered her a glass of water with a slice of lemon, and then they moved into the living room. The light was softer now, slanting through the curtains—the day easing into its second half.

Claire settled into the couch. "There's a weight in your writing," she said. "Not in a bad way. Just…I can feel it. I can feel you've lived it."

Ben sat across from her. He didn't respond right away. He just let her words settle.

"You don't write like someone imagining pain," she said. "You write like someone who's walked through it."

He nodded slowly. "I have. Not your kind of pain. Not what you went through. But…yeah. I know what it's like to feel like you're living in a prison of your own making. I think after my divorce, I didn't just lose my marriage—I lost the version of myself I thought I'd become. I carried that for years. No one put me in a cell. I built it."

Claire watched him carefully.

"I used to think healing was about forgetting," Ben said. "But the scar doesn't go away. And I don't think it's supposed to. What's different now is…the pain that used to sit in the front seat? It's not even in the car anymore."

Claire smiled, eyes shining. "That's it, Ben. That's what you put in the book. That's what people need to hear. Those aren't just your words. That's something God gave you."

Ben looked down for a moment, then back at her.

"They're helping me," she said. "I think they'll help others too."

He smiled. Nothing grand. Just a quiet expression of something deepening in him.

And in her.

The afternoon light kept shifting, but neither of them moved.

Not yet.

CHAPTER 21

When the Scar Speaks

A couple more days passed, and Ben's manuscript had crept past forty thousand words. The story was growing—layered now, not just with scenes, but with meaning. Patterns were starting to emerge. Threads he hadn't planned were weaving themselves together in quiet, unexpected ways.

The cursor blinked on the screen. Not impatient. Just steady. Waiting.

Ben sat in his office, fingers resting on the keyboard, eyes distant. He'd already written a few strong pages that morning—honest ones. But now he hovered in that strange in-between, unsure if the next sentence was ready to arrive, or if he was simply afraid of what it might say.

The scar hadn't left his mind—not really. The rock sat quietly on a shelf across the room, untouched for days. He hadn't looked at it in a while. But now, as the cursor pulsed and the morning light stretched across the rug, his thoughts returned to it. Not with urgency. Just presence. He stood, crossed the room, and picked it up. It sat in his palm with the same quiet warmth it always had. The scar ran across its surface like an old thought he hadn't quite finished having.

There was a knock.

Ben opened the door to find Claire standing there, a gentle smile on her face, her hair swept loosely back. She wore jeans and a light sweater, a bag slung over one shoulder—a familiar kind of casual comfortable in his presence now.

"Hope I'm not interrupting," she said.

"You are," Ben replied, grinning gently.

Claire laughed. "Perfect. I figured you could use someone to annoy you."

Ben stepped aside, still smiling. "You're the perfect interruption."

Before stepping fully inside, she leaned forward. Their lips met—this time with more depth than the others. Not hesitant. Not testing. Just present.

It lingered longer, and when they pulled back, there was no awkward glance, no need to explain. Just something mutual. Quiet. Certain.

Ben held up the rock. "You're just in time for a reunion."

Claire followed him into the office, dropping her bag gently to the floor. She slid into the chair beside his desk and looked at the open document on the screen.

"You've been writing about the rock?" she asked. "Are you finding answers?"

He nodded slowly. "I thought I was done with the scar—or at least done trying to figure it out. But it's back."

He turned the rock slowly in his hand before placing it down next to the laptop. Claire glanced at it, then at him.

"Maybe it never left. Maybe you just stopped listening to what it's trying to say."

Ben exhaled, his eyes drifting to the screen. "I think finishing this book scares me more than starting it did."

"Because finishing it means letting it all go?"

"Because then there's nothing left to hide behind. If I finish it, it means I've said what needed saying. And after that, the silence is mine."

She didn't respond immediately. Instead, she scrolled gently through the page, eyes steady.

Her hand stopped. She leaned in slightly, then read the line aloud, softly:

"Sometimes we sing because we believe. Other times, we sing so we don't forget how."

Claire's hand lifted to her mouth for a moment, emotion moving quietly through her.

"That's so powerful, Ben," she said softly. "That line… it carries real weight."

Ben leaned back in his chair, the corner of his mouth lifting. "June said that to me backstage. I didn't understand it back then. Not really. I do now."

She didn't speak—just nodded slightly, her eyes not leaving his. The quiet that followed wasn't awkward. It was reverent.

After a moment, she smiled gently and said, "Maybe we should step outside. Get some air."

Ben stood. "Good idea."

He offered a hand, and she took it. They didn't say more—just walked out onto the deck, the story still resting open on the screen behind them.

The breeze had picked up since morning, cool and carrying the soft scents of cut grass and distant pine. They settled into chairs on the deck, each with a drink in hand, the late-afternoon sun stretched long across the yard. Claire tucked her feet beneath her and stared out toward the trees.

"I know it's not finished," she said after a while. "And I know some parts are still raw. But Ben, I really think it's time Mark saw it."

He didn't answer right away. His gaze lingered on the horizon, where the woods thinned into sky.

"Without an ending?" he asked.

"Especially without one," she said. "That's part of what makes it powerful. It's still becoming. And Mark will see that. So will Natalie."

Ben looked down at his glass, then over to her. "You think they'll get it?"

"I do. And if nothing else, they'll hear the heart of it. That matters more than whether it's polished or perfect."

He nodded slowly. "If he reads it, he'll know it's still in motion."

"I'll make that clear," she said, pulling her phone from her bag. "Dinner this week? We let them read while we eat?"

He hesitated, then smiled. "Let's do it."

She typed out a message, thumb hovering for just a second before she hit send.

Thursday. Ben's place. Six o'clock?

Ben leaned back again, staring upward at the sky now shifting into gold and pink, streaks of color pulled thin across the edges of the clouds.

"Feels like it's getting real."

"It already was," Claire said. "Now it's just being seen."

He looked over at her—her presence calm, settled, but not without its own weight.

"You've helped me more than I know how to say."

"That's mutual," she said. "You didn't fix me, Ben. But you've walked beside me in a way I didn't know I needed. And your words—what you've written aren't just words on a screen. They're healing."

Claire's phone buzzed. She glanced at the screen and smiled.

"It's Natalie. She says, *'Sounds great. Mark and I are looking forward to it.'*"

Ben took her hand in his, his thumb grazing her knuckles.

They sat quietly, the breeze whispering low through the branches above them. No need to fill the silence. It was part of the rhythm now.

Inside, the scarred rock waited beside the laptop, still and familiar.

And the story—unfinished, yes—but alive, moved forward without needing to be pushed.

CHAPTER 22

The Manuscript

Over the next couple of days, Ben tweaked, expanded, and clarified the story. He was nearing fifty-seven thousand words now and feeling cautiously confident that Mark and Natalie would appreciate what he'd done. But time would tell.

Thursday was approaching, and he wanted to be sure he'd done enough to give them a clear sense of what he was trying to say. Still, the absence of an ending gnawed at him more than he wanted to admit. He reminded himself: it didn't need to be finished. Just honest. And what he had now—unfinished as it was—felt closer to whole. At least whole enough to share.

He'd been pacing most of the morning. Not frantically—just that quiet kind of restlessness that moves in loops. The kind that wears a path into the wood floor between the edge of his desk and the window overlooking the front yard.

He wasn't nervous like he used to be before a performance or a book release. This was something deeper. A different kind of vulnerability. The kind that comes when a piece of your soul is about to be held in someone else's hands.

Claire arrived a little after eleven o'clock, carrying a paper bag of still-warm muffins and the calm energy he'd come to expect from her. She didn't knock—just opened the door and stepped into the space like she belonged there. She did. She placed the bag on the counter and studied him for a moment before speaking.

They spent most of the day talking—long walks, quiet moments, and stretches of silence that didn't need filling.

By late afternoon, the shadows had shifted. Ben glanced at the clock. "They'll be here soon."

"You're nervous," she said plainly.

Ben nodded, not even pretending otherwise. "Yeah."

He didn't need to explain. She knew. She moved toward him and gently placed her hand on his chest, right over the place that felt tight.

"You're not afraid they won't like it," she said. "You're afraid it won't matter."

Her words hit like a breath of cold air. He didn't respond. He didn't need to. She was right.

Claire kissed him then—softly, gently—just enough to stop the spinning. When she pulled back, her eyes held his without fear.

"It matters, Ben. Because you matter. And whatever Mark says, it doesn't change that. But I think he's going to see what I see. You've written something real here. Let him see it."

Ben exhaled hard. "They'll be here soon."

As if on cue, the tires of a silver SUV crunched softly in the driveway, the sun catching the windshield as it rolled to a stop. Claire stepped toward the door while Ben stayed back in the hallway, one hand on the doorway frame like it might steady him.

Natalie entered first—sunny, familiar, hugging Claire like a sister. Mark followed, calm and sharp-eyed, carrying a small gift bag with a box of herbal tea and a notebook tucked inside. That was more his style. Practical. Thoughtful.

"We brought something," he said, handing the bag to Ben. "Didn't know if you were still drinking coffee after noon, so this seemed safer."

Ben smiled, grateful for the gesture—less for what was inside, more for what it meant. Mark had shown up. Claire had come early. And somehow, despite the nerves, this moment didn't feel overwhelming. It felt right.

The small talk was easy. They gathered in the kitchen for a few minutes, catching up, sipping iced tea. Claire and Natalie settled into conversation like no time had passed at all. Eventually, Mark glanced toward Ben and tilted his head in the direction of the hallway.

"You ready?"

Ben hesitated, then nodded. "Yeah. Let's go."

They stepped into Ben's office, and the energy shifted. The manuscript was open on the screen—first chapter already loaded, a blinking cursor waiting like a held breath. The room smelled faintly of coffee and lemon oil from the cloth Ben had used to dust earlier. Mark took a seat, pulled the laptop a little closer, and looked at Ben.

"Mind if I read a bit?"

Ben gestured for him to go ahead. "Only if you promise not to blow smoke."

Mark gave a half-smile. "Have I ever?"

Then the room went silent.

Ben stood by the bookshelf, pretending to read the titles. Pretending not to care. But his pulse was racing. Mark scrolled slowly, reading in silence, his expression still and unreadable. Five minutes passed. Then ten. Ben stopped pacing. He watched Mark now—his eyes moving, the subtle shifts in his brow, the occasional narrowing of his gaze.

Finally, Mark leaned back. He didn't speak right away. He let the weight of it hang there, thick and quiet.

"This isn't like your other stuff," he said at last. "Not even close."

Ben tensed slightly. "Too different?"

"No," Mark said. "Better. Raw. Honest. It reads like someone bleeding into the page—not to shock, but to heal. I didn't feel like I was reading a book. I felt like I was being let into something sacred."

Ben looked down, unsure how to hold the weight of the compliment.

"There are a few places I'd tighten," Mark continued, "a couple things I might move. But that's just technical. What matters is how it feels. And Ben…it feels. It made me stop and think. Made me remember some things I hadn't thought about in a long time. That doesn't happen often."

Ben nodded slowly, almost afraid to believe it.

"I didn't write this to get published," he said. "Not this one. I wrote it because I didn't know what else to do with all of it. I wrote it to breathe. To get it out of me before it drove me crazy."

Mark studied him for a moment, then walked toward the window.

"Then that's exactly why it's worth publishing. Because it's not just for you."

Ben frowned. "What do you mean?"

"You're writing for the ones who never picked up the rock," Mark said. "The ones who saw the scar and thought it disqualified them. You're writing for the ones who feel too late, too broken, too forgotten to still matter. But they do. That's what your story says—*they're still called, and it's not too late.*"

Ben felt his throat tighten.

"You're not telling them what to believe," Mark said, voice quiet but certain. "You're showing them what it looks like to believe after you've been broken. And that's something people don't forget. That's what makes it holy."

The room went still again. Ben turned back to the laptop. Still no title. Still no neat ending. But maybe that wasn't the point anymore.

Claire appeared in the doorway, her eyes searching Ben's face. "How'd it go?"

Mark looked over. "He's got something real here."

Claire smiled. "I know."

Mark stood and stretched, then said, "I want Nat to read a few chapters—just to confirm what I think we're all feeling. This isn't just another book, Ben Thomas. This one could really change lives."

Claire called out, and a moment later, Natalie stepped in. She moved to the desk, where the laptop still sat open. Without a word, she began to read. The room stayed quiet except for the wind brushing the window and the slow, rhythmic tick of the clock.

At first, Natalie's face was unreadable. But then her posture shifted. She leaned closer. Her fingers hovered above the keys. Her breath caught.

Then she read aloud, voice soft, steady:

"There's a weight I can't name. It follows me—quiet, steady, familiar. I don't know what it wants from me yet. But I know I have to follow it. Maybe it's not a burden. Maybe it's a calling—something I was meant to carry."

She looked up at Ben, her voice low, thoughtful. "It's strong, Ben. Honest. I can feel there's more coming, but what you've written already…it's compelling. It matters." She paused, then added, "This book is going to be a powerful one."

Ben sank slowly into the chair beside the desk, his eyes moving between them.

"I don't know if I'm ready to call it a book yet," he said. "Not until I can find an ending."

"You don't have to," Mark replied. "But I'd be honored to help shape it when you are. Because this isn't just a story. It's something that heals—not with noise, but in small, quiet ways. Like a scar no longer hidden. I'm confident the ending will come."

Natalie closed the laptop gently and sat back, as if holding something fragile inside her. No one rushed to speak. The room, full of layered silence, felt like the kind that followed prayer—or maybe became one.

Claire glanced at Ben and gave a small, knowing smile. "Dinner's waiting."

They moved into the kitchen, plates already set, the roast warm, the salad dressed, bread still soft from the oven. They ate slowly, conversation moving between family, music, Claire's daughter, Natalie's latest editing project, and Mark's half-finished woodworking bench in the garage.

No one pushed the topic of the manuscript. It didn't need pushing. It was in the room, in the air between them, present even in the laughter that surfaced now and then.

By the time the sun had dipped behind the trees and dusk had settled, they stood on the porch, saying their goodbyes. Natalie hugged Claire tightly. Mark shook Ben's hand, then paused.

"Think about it," he said. "I meant what I said. I'd be honored to help shape this. You've already done the hard part."

Ben nodded. "I'll consider it. I promise."

As their car pulled away, Ben stood at the edge of the porch with Claire beside him. The night had settled in soft and deep, the kind that didn't need filling. They didn't speak. They didn't need to.

The house behind them was quiet. But something in Ben's heart had shifted—like a door that had stayed shut for too long...slowly beginning to open.

CHAPTER 23

The Unexpected Lunch Break

Ben didn't write that morning. The manuscript sat untouched on the laptop—several chapters deep, unfinished. Still no ending. But maybe it would come soon.

Strangely, that unknown didn't bother him the way it had been before.

The meeting with Mark had stirred something in him—gratitude, doubt, maybe even hope. He still wasn't sure if he was writing a book for others or a letter to himself. He didn't know if he'd ever fully understand the rock, or the scar, or how any of this had really begun.

He didn't need it all to make sense.

He just wanted it to matter.

A buzz from his phone broke the silence. A message from Claire: *What are you doing today? Lunch at my place?*

He smiled and texted back: *I'd love that. Want me to bring anything?*

Just yourself.

Perfect. I'll see you around noon.

The drive was quiet. Trees passed in a blur of green and gold, and his thoughts drifted just as easily from the book, to Claire, to the sense that none of this had been accidental. God's hand was in it. Of that, he was certain. Not everything needed a sign when peace had already settled in.

Ben tapped the steering wheel in rhythm with the road. A soft instrumental played low on the stereo—something he hadn't listened to in years, yet somehow it felt like it belonged to this chapter of his life. He caught his reflection in the rearview mirror: calm eyes, a faint smile. He looked different. Maybe not healed, but less hollow. Less haunted.

The streets began to feel familiar. The corner store with the crooked sign. The curve in the road where trees reached overhead like a cathedral. Nothing remarkable, yet today it all felt quietly alive. Subtle reminders that the world wasn't just functioning, it was flourishing. And maybe, in some small way, so was he.

He thought about Claire—her voice, the way she tilted her head when something truly mattered, the quiet steadiness she carried into every room. Just the idea of seeing her made his chest tighten and ease at the same time. A thought flickered: *What if she's the one?* The idea made him nervous. But it made him smile, too. Maybe he was getting ahead of himself. Or maybe he was just finally catching up to the part of his heart that still believed love was possible.

As he neared her house, he felt it—the anticipation, the warmth. Maybe today he'd tell her how much she meant to him.

Claire opened the door with a hug. Her hair was pulled back, and she wore a soft, pale-blue sweater. Familiar. Comfortable.

"Lemonade?" she asked. "Come sit on the porch. It's nice out."

He followed her outside. But something in her voice had shifted—not harsh, but tight. Tense.

They sat. She handed him a glass and took a breath.

"Have you written anything new?"

Ben shook his head. "Not today. Still stuck on the ending. I'm thinking about Mark's offer, but…I'm not sure."

Claire nodded, her eyes drifting toward the trees. Her fingers tapped softly against the glass. Then she turned to him, voice low but clear.

"Ben, I need to tell you something."

His chest tightened. "Okay."

She looked down, then met his eyes. "You're one of the best men I've met in a long time. Truly. And I haven't dated much since moving from Chicago. But after last night—the dinner, the reading, the drive home—I started to feel scared."

He stayed quiet. Just listened.

"Not of you," she added quickly. "Not of what's happened so far. But scared of what might happen if we keep going. I don't want to ruin something good. I don't want to move too fast into something I'm not ready for."

He exhaled slowly. The silence stretched.

"I care about you, Ben. I really do. And I want to keep getting to know you. But there's something in me that's holding back. I don't even fully know why. I just know…I need a little space. Not forever. Just enough to breathe."

He nodded slowly. The sting found its place.

"This kind of caught me off guard," he said quietly.

"I know." Her voice wavered. Tears welled, but she didn't look away. "And I hated thinking about having to say it. But I couldn't pretend."

Ben stood, then sat again, unsure what to do with his hands or his heart.

"I care about you too," he said. "More than I expected to. And yeah…I'm afraid too. But I don't want to lose what we've started."

She reached over and gently took his hand.

"Then don't lose it. Just let it pause. Let me catch up."

He nodded again—this time not in agreement, but in surrender.

"Okay."

They hugged—a long, slow moment neither of them could name. She kissed his cheek.

"You're a good man, Ben. Keep writing. Keep searching."

He gave her a faint smile. "I will."

The drive home blurred past. He didn't remember the turns. Didn't remember walking through the front door. He just stood in the hallway, keys in hand, wondering what had shifted beneath him.

That night, he didn't open the manuscript. Didn't journal. Didn't search for answers the usual way. He simply prayed—quietly, without flourish—and let the stillness take him under.

If this is a nightmare, he thought, *I'd like to wake up now.*

But it wasn't. This was real. This was life.

He'd been here before. Not this exact moment, but this ache. It felt like an old record—stuck on the same few lines, repeating until the song lost meaning.

Still, he tried to hold on to something. Claire hadn't ended it. She hadn't closed the door. She'd asked him to wait.

But patience had never been his strength.

"Why can't this just work?" he whispered. To the room. To the ceiling. Maybe even to the rock still sitting quietly on the shelf—unmoved but not forgotten.

No answer came. Only silence.

And in that silence, he lay still—hoping that despite everything, hope hadn't walked out the door with her.

Just then, his phone buzzed.

A text from Eric: *Dad, quick question. Do you remember what bait you used during the tournament last year to catch that monster bass?*

It was completely random—but maybe that's what he needed. A gentle interruption. A reminder of life, and what he still had.

He texted back: *I think it was a red flake green pumpkin jig. That's the one I used when I caught the six-pounder that got us into the money.*

Eric replied: *That's what I thought. I'm headed there this weekend to fish—wanted to try the same spot.*

Ben smiled. *Good luck. Hope you catch a big one.*

He sat with the phone in his hand, thinking how a simple message from his son had eased the ache—just a little.

Then he thought of Melody. He hadn't heard from her in a few days, so he sent a quick text: *I'm lucky to have you as my daughter. Eric just texted—he's going fishing. Got me thinking how blessed I am to have kids who love life...and love me. Love you, Mel. Tell the kids hi.*

Melody replied a moment later: *Thanks, Dad. Love you too.*

Ben sat back and just breathed.

He wasn't sure what would happen with Claire. But for now, he knew this much:

He was still a blessed man. But he had more questions than answers.

CHAPTER 24

Time to Go Back

The next few days were heavy—quiet on the outside, but loud in his mind. Ben kept circling the same old questions, the ones he thought he'd finally laid to rest before that first trip to Ilwaco. But now they returned—relentless, familiar. *Have I missed something with God? Have I stepped outside the lines again, made a wrong turn without even seeing it? Am I cursed and have to carry this weight forever, always just shy of something real?*

He couldn't stop thinking about Claire. About their conversations in Lincoln City, the walks, the dinners, the honesty. He hadn't gone to the coast looking for someone like her. He hadn't gone looking for anyone.

But then she appeared—like something written in.

And now? Now it felt like she was slipping through his fingers just as she'd started to matter.

He reached for his phone and typed a quick message to Claire: *Hope you're doing well. Hope you're healing—or sorting out whatever you need. I'm here. No pressure. Just wanted to say hi.*

He set the phone down and looked toward his desk—then at the rock. He knew he needed to keep moving.

He hadn't opened his laptop in three days. Hadn't written a word. The manuscript sat untouched, the cursor frozen mid-sentence like it was waiting for him to breathe again.

Just as he started to doze off, his phone buzzed. He grabbed it too quickly.

It wasn't Claire.

It was Josh.

Hey, random question—do you still have that old amp I loaned you years ago? I swear I saw it in a photo the other day. No rush, just curious.

Ben replied: *Pretty sure it's still in the garage. Want me to dig it out?*

Nah, no rush. Just one of those things that popped into my head. Hope you're doing okay, man.

Thanks. You too.

But the truth sat quietly in his chest. He'd been hoping it was Claire.

Then his phone buzzed again. This time it was Mark.

Hey, Ben, you find an ending to the book yet? I'm ready when you are. Let me know.

Ben sent a quick reply.

No, nothing yet.

He didn't mention Claire. Didn't say he hadn't opened the laptop in days. He wasn't ready to talk about any of that.

He stood there a moment longer, wondering: *Is this it? Is the story already over?* The book was so close, but his heart was aching again—that old, familiar ache. He didn't know why life had to be so difficult sometimes. But even in the fog, he felt the nudge: *keep going.* He didn't need every answer. But he did need an ending. And maybe, just maybe, that ending still waited for him—out there.

Somewhere in the mystery of that rock.

He walked to the bathroom, splashed water on his face, stared at himself in the mirror. He had to get a grip. He could spiral now, let this pain bury him—or he could stand up and move. Claire had told him not to stop writing—not to stop searching.

He knew what he needed to do.

Ilwaco.

He grabbed a small bag and packed light. Tucked the rock into his jacket pocket, where it felt heavier than he remembered. He stepped outside. The Corvette's engine rumbled to life—a sound he hadn't heard in weeks. The old beast still had something to say, and so did he.

He drove through the familiar backroads first—slow stretches of farmland, two-lane blacktops lined with bare trees and weathered fences. Towns passed like old postcards: faded diners, quiet intersections, gas stations with flickering signs. It was hours before the air began to shift.

Then, as the road began to curve and the terrain grew wilder, he caught the scent of salt on the wind. The coast was still miles out, but he could feel it getting closer. The ache in his chest didn't lift, but something steadied.

By the time he reached the coastal highway, the sky had begun to soften. The road twisted along the cliffs like a half-forgotten ribbon. And finally, the sea came into view—wide and endless, breathing in slow rhythm beside him.

There was no music. No noise. Just the road, and the ache he was carrying back toward its origin.

He arrived late, just as the sky began to bruise. The same old motel had a vacancy sign glowing faintly. He checked in, dropped his bag, placed the rock on the small table by the window, and stared at it for a long time.

He realized he was trying to recreate it—whatever *it* was. That first time. The spark. The feeling. The meaning. But too much had changed. *He* had changed.

Never in a million years had he expected to be back here again—at least not this soon. And not like this.

He sat, laptop closed beside him, notebook in hand just in case. But he didn't write. He just stared. Thought of Claire. Wondered if she was thinking of him too.

His phone buzzed.

He looked down, heart stuttering.

It was her.

Hey. Thanks for the message. I'm still here. Just need some space. —Claire

Ben let the screen go dark. No reply needed. That message *was* the reply. A quiet reassurance, nothing more, nothing less. She wasn't gone. But she wasn't ready. Life didn't promise anything—not even tomorrow.

He didn't understand all of it. Didn't understand the pain. But something inside him was still reaching. Still listening.

Night fell. His body was worn down by everything the days had carried. The bed was stiff, but he welcomed it. Closed his eyes, mind still spinning.

Then, a thought struck.

Maybe I was never supposed to take the rock home.

Maybe that was the mistake. Maybe he'd disrupted something by removing it from where it belonged. Like trying to carry a symbol meant to stay rooted. Maybe the answer wasn't in holding on—but in *returning* what wasn't his to keep.

He whispered into the dark, "I'll bring it back."

Ben stood, quiet but certain, and slid the rock into the pocket of the jacket hanging over the chair.

Tomorrow, I will rise. I will walk it back to the beach—to the exact spot where it had found me—and put it back.

And maybe then—just maybe—the rest of the story will begin to make sense.

CHAPTER 25

The Restless Room

Ben couldn't sleep.

Not for lack of trying. He'd laid still for hours, body sunk into the creaky motel mattress, the smell of old fabric and faint coffee lingering in the air. His eyes stayed closed even after it became clear they weren't going to stay that way. Something in him was too alert. Too full. Like the day had poured in and refused to drain out.

The room was quiet—not peaceful quiet but waiting quiet. The kind that settles like dust in the corners of an attic you're not supposed to enter. Still, but watchful.

He rolled onto his side, then onto his back. The pillow went from too flat to too thick with nothing in between. The blanket tangled around his legs like a wire that wouldn't give. No position felt like rest. And when he finally sat up, the motion wasn't frustration; it was surrender.

He rubbed his face with both hands. The cold air touched the sweat at his temples and made him shiver. His chest felt heavy—not with panic or dread, but something older. Something unfinished.

He stood and crossed the room slowly, every step softened by worn carpet. The motel was utterly still. No creaking walls, no plumbing groans. Just the hum of the mini-fridge and the occasional click of the heater trying to matter.

He pulled the rock from his pocket and let it rest in his hand. The warmth hadn't faded. It was just as it had been when he first picked it up—quiet, steady, alive.

The scar hadn't changed either, but it looked sharper somehow. Cleaner. As if the light had figured out how to see it properly. The groove curved slightly upward—not dramatic, not deep—but sure. He ran his thumb across it. It pushed back, just enough to say, *"I'm still here."*

Ben sat in the chair, elbows resting on his knees, both hands cupping the rock like a question too big to ask out loud.

He wasn't trying to figure anything out. Not anymore. He just needed to be with it. With the scar. With the warmth. With the weight that had followed him into this night and refused to let go.

Outside the window, the motel sign flickered in slow arguments with the dark. A few letters had given up long ago. The light barely reached the edge of the gravel lot, where shadows stretched across the dunes. And somewhere past the dunes, the ocean breathed.

He could hear it now—low and steady, the world exhaling again and again. Normally that rhythm brought comfort. Tonight, it felt like a warning. Or a countdown. Or a summons.

And then—it happened.

Not a sound. Not a flash. Just a shift.

The air changed first—heavier, but quieter. Everything turned inward. The light from the lamp didn't flicker, but the corners of the room began to blur. The walls dimmed. The ceiling let go. The carpet beneath his feet didn't vanish. It just stopped mattering.

The room receded.

He didn't close his eyes, but it felt like the world did. There was no motion. No dizziness. No sound. Just the sense that something else had opened. Something old. Something real.

The rock in his hands remained solid. Its warmth steadied him. It became the only anchor in a place that no longer had shape.

Light filled the space—not from above or around, but from everywhere. From within. Not harsh. Not radiant. But alive. It wasn't there to show him anything. It was there to hold him.

And he was not alone.

He saw no face. No silhouette. But presence filled the space like gravity. It didn't move toward him. It already *was* there. And it saw him.

Not his posture. Not his body. *Him.*

All of him. The whole of his life laid bare—not invasive, not cruel—just true. He didn't feel judged. He didn't feel affirmed either. He felt *known.* As though the scar in the stone had found its echo inside his chest and whispered, *"There you are."*

He tried to speak, but words dissolved before they reached his throat. Language had no use here.

Time didn't pass. Or maybe it did and simply refused to say so.

Then, slowly, gently, the light withdrew. Not in a flash. Not in a closing door. It faded like fog lifting off cold sand. The air returned. The walls returned. The room rebuilt itself around him like someone reassembling it from memory.

The table was beneath his elbows again. The chair creaked beneath his weight. The lamp buzzed faintly. The mini-fridge resumed its hum.

He was back.

Still holding the rock. Still tracing the scar. Still changed.

He looked around. Everything appeared exactly as it had. But none of it felt untouched.

The silence wasn't empty anymore. It was full. Full of what, he didn't know.

His coffee sat cold on the desk. His laptop waited, closed but not forgotten. Outside, the ocean kept breathing. The night held its shape.

But he didn't move. Not yet.

The rock rested in his hands, its warmth unchanged. The scar steady beneath his thumb.

And though no voice had spoken, though no vision had declared its meaning, Ben knew one thing for certain:

Something had begun. And whatever it was, it would not leave him untouched.

CHAPTER 26

The Unexplainable Moment

Morning came late.

Gray light seeped through the blinds in thin, uncertain strands—like even the sun wasn't sure it should rise. The air felt heavier than it had the night before. Still, quiet, but not peaceful. The stillness had an edge now, like something had shifted while the world slept.

Ben stirred in the chair, stiff from the way he'd folded into himself during the night. His neck ached, and the side of his face bore the imprint of the jacket collar where he'd rested. He blinked against the dimness, unsure whether he'd slept an hour or not at all. The heater had stopped sometime in the dark, and the air carried a chill that didn't feel entirely physical.

He looked over at the nightstand.

The rock sat exactly where he'd left it after whatever had passed through the night—undisturbed, silent, as if it had been waiting all along.

He stared at it for a long time.

The scar drew his eye again. Not an accident of erosion. Not natural. He could feel it, just like before. Not just in his hand—but in his chest. In his breath. Like the mark had memory. Like it was waking something up in him.

He didn't want to pick it up.

But he already had.

His fingers closed around it. The warmth was immediate, deeper than before. Not hot. But alive. A pulse, steady and slow, like a second heartbeat. And when his thumb brushed the scar, something inside him tightened—like a string pulled taut across the soul.

His eyes closed. He didn't mean to. It just… happened.

And with that breath, the motel thinned.

No spinning. No flash of light. Just…absence.

The chair, the heater, the hum of the mini-fridge—all vanished like breath on glass. Not erased. Just irrelevant.

He wasn't dreaming.

He was somewhere else.

The ground beneath him was hard. Packed dirt. Cold. The air carried dust and blood and something older than either.

He stood at the edge of a narrow street—walled on both sides by stone buildings from a different time that leaned inward. The sky overhead was dim, the light bruised. There were no people. No sound. Just wind.

He looked down. The rock was still in his hand.

But the scar was glowing.

A dull red, like embers that refused to die. He turned his hand. The groove in the stone throbbed, and for a moment—just a moment—he felt it throb in his own body too. In his chest. In a place where sorrow and wonder meet.

Then came the first sound.

Footsteps.

Slow. Dragging. Heavy.

Ben turned toward it instinctively.

From the far end of the narrow street, a figure emerged.

Barefoot. Bent. Carrying something enormous across His back. A beam of wood—rough, splintered, dark with sweat and dirt. His skin was torn across the shoulders. Strips of cloth clung to His frame, soaked and clinging.

His face was down, obscured beneath tangled hair, blood, and the angle of the beam across His back. He didn't speak, didn't groan, didn't plead. He simply moved forward, slow and deliberate, with the weight of the wood forcing Him into a posture no man would choose. Something instinctive pulled Ben backward, tucking him into a shadowed alcove beside the narrow street. He didn't know why. He only knew he wasn't meant to be seen. Not here. Not now.

Ben knew who this man was—Jesus. But how could this be possible? He tried to wake, but the moment held him fast and refused to let go. Then Jesus passed within feet of him. Ben didn't breathe. His hands went cold, even as the scarred stone in his hand stayed warm—too warm. Every muscle in his body tensed, as if it were his own shoulders breaking beneath the weight. He could smell the dirt. The blood. The heat rising off broken skin.

And then, just as Jesus moved past, He lifted His head—not all the way, not with effort, just a small turn of the eyes. Not toward Ben exactly, but through him. And in that flicker, something passed between them. No word. No thought. Just pain. Shared. Unbearable. Sacred. The kind that doesn't ask for understanding. It simply exists—and demands reverence.

Ben wanted to cry out. To fall to his knees. To whisper something, anything. But he didn't move. Couldn't. The air was too thick, his chest too full, the moment too holy. He stayed still, silent, as Jesus turned a corner and disappeared from view. The sound of footsteps faded, swallowed by the silence of that ancient street.

The wind exhaled, and Ben was alone again.

His breath came ragged—not from fear, but recognition. Not intellectual, but deeper. Embodied. His heart didn't race; it pounded—heavy, deliberate, with something undeniable. He didn't need to speak the name aloud. He had known who it was even before Jesus looked up. The scar in the rock had burned—not with anger, but with purpose. It hadn't summoned him as punishment. It had invited him as a witness.

Ben looked down at his hand. The glow from the rock had faded now. The warmth remained, but it had changed—less urgent, more steady. He wrapped his fingers around it, and as he did, the vision began to dissolve. Not violently. It simply unraveled. The street fell away. The wind stilled. The stone walls dissolved like mist, giving way to cheap motel blinds and the pale gray light of coastal Washington.

He was back.

But something wasn't.

A part of him was still there—on that path, in that silence, standing next to Jesus, bent beneath the unbearable weight of mercy. He sat in the chair, the rock in his hand, and stared at the wall like it might open again. He didn't speak. Not yet. No words were large enough to fill the space that moment had opened.

Something had begun. He could feel it.

Not a memory. Not a metaphor. A scar.

And it wasn't his alone.

CHAPTER 27

Toward the Hill

Ben hadn't moved. Not really. After the vision—if that's what it was—he'd returned to the chair like a man sleepwalking. The motel walls had reassembled around him, but the world didn't feel solid yet. His breath had returned. His body had cooled. But his hand still held the rock.

He hadn't set it down. Couldn't. Not after what he'd seen. The warmth pulsed softer now, like something waiting—unfinished, not done speaking.

He thought the moment had passed. That maybe what needed to be shown had been shown, and he could finally take the rock back to its resting place. But something in his chest said otherwise. A pressure. A pull. Whatever had begun…wasn't over.

He sat forward slowly, the weight of the rock still pressing into his palm.

And the scar pulsed once more.

And the room let go.

It didn't fade this time. It yielded.

There was no wind. No sound. No warning. Just a single, fluid moment—and then he was gone.

Not lifted.

Placed.

The ground beneath him was dry and cracked. He stood barefoot, the dirt hot under his heels, the sky above him wide and without mercy. The air smelled of sweat, sunbaked earth, and blood. There were no trees. No shadows. Only the dull shimmer of heat rising off the rocks and the broken hush of something heavy being endured.

He stood on the edge of a hill.

Not a mountain. Not a battlefield.

But it felt like both.

He didn't know how he got there. He didn't ask. The questions had become irrelevant. Only the ache remained—and the knowledge that something holy was happening, and he had been invited not to understand, but to witness.

Ahead of him, maybe thirty paces, the procession moved.

Three men. Soldiers. A beam of wood.

And Jesus.

The same pain he had seen in the alleyway. The same bent frame. The same silence graced with humility.

The blood soaked into His garment. The lashes across His back. The weight of the crossbar biting into muscle and bone. The way His knees buckled every few steps, not from drama, but depletion.

Ben took a step forward, heart pounding. He didn't think about what he was doing. He simply moved. Drawn. Called. Not by sound, but by suffering.

The hill was steep, the dirt dry and powdery, slipping under his steps. He stumbled once, caught himself, pressed on. The sun beat down without shame. The sky had no clouds. The silence of the crowd was deafening.

They were there, scattered along the slope—men, women, and even children. Faces hard. Faces grieving. Faces turned away. No one spoke. No one moved.

Ben reached the edge of the path and stopped. Just beyond, Jesus collapsed beneath the weight of the beam, face buried in the dirt. The soldiers shouted something, gestured wildly.

One of them grabbed His shoulder and yanked. There was no resistance. No cry of protest. Jesus simply turned, slow and steady, not in submission but in surrender. It was not the surrender of weakness, but of will. A decision made long before this moment. A yielding that carried the gravity of eternity.

And then their eyes met.

Not in passing. Not in coincidence. In purpose.

For one suspended second, time held its breath. There was no crowd, no sun, no soldiers—only that gaze. Not sharp. Not accusing. Just present.

Ben felt it press into him like weight without mass. He saw no lightning. Heard no voice. But in those eyes, he knew. Knew with the kind of knowing that breaks a man clean in half. This was no stranger. No metaphor. No symbol carved into stained glass or spoken of in creeds. This was the Son. A man with skin and blood and breath. A man carrying not just wood, but the ache of a thousand lifetimes. A man walking willingly into the unthinkable.

And in His eyes—God help him—Ben saw pain, yes. But not only pain. There was resolve. There was compassion. And there was a silence deeper than any prayer Ben had ever spoken, deeper than language, deeper than guilt. It was a silence that knew everything and held it anyway.

The weight of every wound Ben had ever carried seemed to rise to meet that gaze—his failures, his fears, the quiet regrets he never gave voice to. It all rose to the surface like iron to a magnet. And it wasn't crushed.

It was seen.

Ben dropped to his knees. Not from weakness. Not from ritual. But in reverence. In surrender. In gravity. The scarred stone in his hand pulsed with such heat it felt alive, searing into his palm—not in punishment, but in recognition. This scar was no longer a mystery. It was a door. A witness. A mirror.

He bowed his head, eyes flooding, unable to bear the weight of that sacred stare. His tears darkened the dust at his feet. He let them fall. He didn't beg for mercy. He didn't ask to understand. He only knelt in the presence of the One Who had carried what Ben never could—and did it without bitterness, without pride, without demanding anything in return.

And then, gently, the scene began to unravel.

The hill softened at the edges. The sounds faded into stillness. The heat withdrew like a tide. The crowd, the light, the sky itself—all dissolved without spectacle or warning, as if it had only ever existed in the space between one breath and the next.

He was back in the motel.

Knees pressed into cheap carpet. Hands clenched around a stone that no longer burned, but still pulsed faintly, as if its heart had not finished speaking. The silence in the room was profound. Not empty. Full—full of something that now lived inside him.

Ben stayed there for a long time.

He sat back slowly, wiped his face with the back of his sleeve, and looked toward the window. There was no ocean in sight—just the parking lot, a crooked sign buzzing faintly, and the gray light of another coastal morning. The world had not changed.

But he had.

He didn't know what would come next. He didn't know if the scarred rock would lead him somewhere darker or brighter. He didn't know if this was just the beginning or already too much. But one thing had settled in him with the certainty of gravity.

He had seen Jesus.

He had seen the scar.

And now—whether he was ready—he was witnessing this for a reason.

CHAPTER 28

The Hill Called Skull

Ben was only back for what seemed like a minute, maybe two, and then came the pull—again.

He had never felt fear and confusion like this.

Not the kind that made you run or hide—but the kind that made you stop. That made you realize you were about to stand in a place where no one walked unchanged. It wasn't fear of pain or mystery. It was fear of holiness. The kind of terror that only comes when you begin to understand that something far greater than yourself is reaching toward you—and you are entirely unworthy to stand in its light.

The scarred stone in his palm was already warm. He hadn't even set it down yet.

It lay in the palm of his hand, quiet, still, pulsing faintly in the gray motel light.

He felt it pulling him back—not because he wanted to, but because he had no choice. It was time.

As his fingers wrapped around the rock, the warmth deepened. Not burning. Not sharp. Just steady. Like breath. Like blood moving through veins. The scar beneath his thumb no longer felt foreign. It felt…known. Like it belonged to him. Or maybe he belonged to it.

The room didn't vanish this time.

It surrendered.

And Ben stepped through.

He was on the hill before he even knew he had arrived.

The ground was dry and broken. The sky overhead was bruised and low. The crowd had already gathered—some standing, some kneeling, some shouting, some silent. Soldiers barked orders with flat voices, their hands red and unbothered. Women wept in the shadows. Men looked away. Some laughed.

The wind carried dust and blood and something deeper than both—something that grieved.

Ben stood near the back. He didn't try to move forward. He didn't need to. The moment came to him.

Three crosses had already been raised. Two of them held men writhing in the agony of their own judgment—gasping, cursing, clinging to breath like it could somehow buy them a few more moments of delay. Their flesh was torn, their eyes wild, their pain desperate. But the third cross—the one in the center—held something entirely different. It held a man whose agony was not just physical, but eternal. A man whose body sagged under the weight of something heavier than wood. His arms stretched wide, nailed into ancient timber. His head hung forward, chin against chest, blood streaking down from his scalp, his wrists, his side, his back. Every breath he took was a burden deeper than Ben could ever understand. Slow. Trembling. Nearly impossible.

Ben didn't move. He didn't speak. He couldn't. Nothing in him dared to interrupt the stillness rising inside his chest. Fear was not what held him; it was reverence. He had stepped into something holy, and no words were fit for the air he now breathed.

Jesus was on the cross. He was not screaming. He was not raging against his fate. He was not resisting the injustice of it. He was giving. Giving Himself away with every exhale. Giving love through every ragged breath. Giving forgiveness with every drop of blood that fell to the dust. And somehow, standing there among the crowd, Ben felt as though the gift was not general. It was personal. Intimate. Specific.

He wanted to look away. His mind told him to. His body begged him to. But he couldn't. Something in the stillness— something sacred—held him where he was. He felt as if an invisible thread ran from the foot of the cross to the center of his chest, tethering him to the agony unfolding just above him. He could hear the breathing now. That was what undid him—not the nails, not the hammer, not the mocking voices around him. It was the sound of Jesus' gasping for air. Each breath drawn not in rage, but in mercy. A choice. A deliberate climb into death so that someone else might live.

Ben's knees weakened beneath him, but he stayed upright, held not by strength but by something greater. The scarred stone in his palm began to blaze—not with torment, but with truth. In that moment, he understood. The scar was not an ornament nor a metaphor. It was evidence. Proof that pain had been endured, love had been proven, and a body had been broken—not by accident, not by force, but by choice.

Then Jesus lifted his head.

Slowly. As if raising the entire weight of the world with it.

His eyes swept the crowd—not with condemnation, but with compassion. He wasn't measuring who deserved what. He wasn't counting sins or weighing hearts. He was simply seeing. And in that seeing, he found Ben.

The gaze didn't linger longer than any other. It didn't freeze time. It didn't make the world stop spinning.

But it found him.

And in that single moment, Ben knew.

This was for me.

Not in theory. Not in poetry. Not in some vague theological way you could tuck into a sermon or file under belief. No—this was for him. For the weight he carried. For the nights he lay awake wondering if grace was still possible. For every scar he'd tried to bury. Every wound he refused to name. For the questions. For the silence. For the guilt. For the aching love he felt for his children. For the things he wished he could undo. For the man he was—and the man he wasn't.

It was all there.

Carried. Covered. Crucified. Redeemed.

Ben couldn't breathe. His lungs felt too small to hold the fullness of what was being offered. The sky above began to darken—not like a storm rolling in, but like the veil of heaven itself had started to close. Shadows lengthened. The light bent. And then, from the center of it all, came a voice—not loud, but unignorable.

"Father… forgive them."

The words broke through the silence like thunder wrapped in gentleness. They shattered Ben's heart into a million tiny pieces—not just for the forgiveness being offered, but for the God Who was offering it. No anger was in that voice. No vengeance. Only love. Undeserved. Unearned. And yet freely given.

Ben dropped to his knees.

His hands sank into the dirt, the stone in his palm glowing now with a fierce, quiet fire. The scar wasn't a mark anymore. It was a doorway. A witness. A mirror. It was every moment he had failed to believe he was worth redeeming— and every answer to that doubt.

His head bowed. His shoulders trembled. The tears came—not in a torrent, but in surrender. No prayers were on his lips. No confessions. Just sound. The sound of a soul finally breaking open—not in despair, but in awe. His heart was being healed by the sacrifice, by the scar—not the one on the rock, but the ones Jesus bore.

Above him, the sky turned black. The earth trembled with a low, aching groan. Jesus hung on the cross and gasped one final cry—a sound so filled with agony and authority that it seemed to shake the very structure of time.

And then it was finished.

The darkness fell fully.

And Ben was gone—back in the motel.

CHAPTER 29

The Weight that Remained

Ben didn't stand right away.

The motel room held a hush that felt deeper than silence, as if it had absorbed something sacred and didn't yet know what to do with it. He stayed on his knees for a long time, his hands wrapped around the rock, his head bowed—not in ritual, but in reverence. The scar in his palm had cooled, but its echo remained, pulsing somewhere beneath skin and memory.

He had seen Jesus.

Not in a stained-glass way. Not through parables or Sunday verses. He had stood within reach of the crossbar, close enough to smell the blood, to hear the breathlessness of suffering. He had watched Him fall, watched Him carry, watched Him look—not at the crowd, but into Ben. Through

Ben. As if He'd known every failure, every hidden fear, every half-hearted prayer—and still didn't look away.

Ben had never felt more unworthy. Or more loved.

And now, he was back in a room that smelled like motel soap and dust and yesterday's coffee. The blinds stirred faintly in the draft from the window. The carpet beneath his knees was rough. The scarred rock was still warm in his hand.

Slowly, he pushed himself upright, legs stiff. He eased into the chair, the frame creaking beneath him as he leaned back—like a man just learning how to breathe again.

There were no visions now. No flickers of light. No disorienting transport to the edge of some ancient street. Just the quiet of a room that had waited for him. Just the steady rhythm of his own breath, no longer afraid.

He exhaled and let the silence hold him.

He knew the story didn't end there.

The cross wasn't the conclusion; it was the hinge. The pivot in history that turned death into something powerless. Ben hadn't seen the empty tomb. He hadn't witnessed the stone rolled away or the linen folded where the body had been. But he didn't need to. He knew.

Jesus had risen.

He'd always known that, of course. It had been said to him, sung to him, etched into his theology like a watermark. But this was different. Now it lived in him—not as knowledge, but as presence. The kind of knowing that couldn't be dissected or diagrammed. It just was.

He imagined the aftermath—the hill, the silence, the torn veil, the stunned sky. He thought of Mary, of Peter, of the others who saw Him again. Who touched the risen scars and heard the same voice call them by name.

And something inside Ben ached for a moment still to come—maybe even hoped that the rock, or God, or whatever this was, might take him back one more time to that moment in history.

But something calm within made him gently aware: he had seen what God had allowed him to see. The vision had come to an end—not by force, but by grace.

He longed to see His face again—not as escape, not as reward, but as reunion. A meeting long promised and suddenly more alive than ever.

He stood, carefully, letting his body find balance again. The rock slipped into his jacket pocket like it belonged there. The weight of it felt right—not as a burden, but as a reminder.

The day outside was gray. The sky undecided. But the air had shifted.

He poured a fresh cup of motel coffee—watery and bitter—but drank it anyway. He didn't need it to taste good. He simply needed something warm in his hands while the rest of him thawed from whatever fire he'd just walked through.

He didn't write yet. Didn't journal. Didn't try to explain. He just stood for a while, listening to the faint hum of the heater, the distant cry of a seagull, the slow tick of the wall clock.

Ilwaco had given him more than clarity. It had given him communion.

It hadn't answered every question. But it had quieted the ones that didn't matter. It had hollowed him out in a way that didn't leave him empty—but expectant. Made room for something he hadn't known how to ask for.

Not relief. Not even peace.

Calling.

The ache inside him had found a voice. The scar had opened something real. And the road ahead, uncertain as it was, had begun to shine with purpose.

He looked once more out the window.

Ilwaco hadn't healed him.

Jesus had.

And now the world—the real, pulsing, fog-swept world—was still there. Unchanged. But Ben wasn't. Something had shifted. Not fully understood. Not yet named. But present. Settling into him like breath after a long silence.

He stayed by the window longer than he meant to. The motel room had grown dim, washed in the blue-gray light of a coast that rarely slept but never rushed. The rock in his jacket still warm, its presence as steady as the hush inside him.

And then—finally—he understood: The rock had never held power. It had only been a stone.

But God had used it.

God had spoken through a rock—not in audible words, not with spectacle or magic—but in a way Ben couldn't explain and no longer needed to. Not for the rock's sake, but for his.

It wasn't about the object. It never had been.

It was grace—wrapped in something small enough to hold, and deep enough to break him open.

He smiled. How long he'd spent trying to understand the symbol instead of surrendering to the Source. He had searched the scar for meaning. But the message had been in the mercy all along.

The encounter. The forgiveness. The voice that had met him in silence.

That was the miracle.

Not the rock. Not the warmth.

The scarred stone in his palm wasn't the proof. The healing in his soul was.

He hadn't spoken aloud in hours, but the silence hadn't been empty. It had been full—crowded, even—with something that lingered beyond words. What he'd seen, what he'd carried, what he now knew…pulsed beneath the surface like the tide. Like breath. Like memory that refused to be boxed away.

He hadn't left the room since returning from the hill. Not really. He'd stood in the same spot for what felt like forever, letting it all wash over him again and again—the lashes, the beam, the eyes that had met his without judgment, without blame, but with a love so fierce it undid him. The ache in his chest hadn't faded, but it had changed. What had once felt like confusion, longing, regret—now felt like reverence. Gravity. Purpose.

He turned away from the window, slow and quiet, and sat on the edge of the bed. His jacket was still draped over the chair, the Bible from the nightstand untouched. The heater clicked once and fell silent. Outside, the wind pushed against the edges of the building but couldn't get in.

Not here. Not tonight.

He didn't reach for the rock again. It was already tucked in his jacket, the weight of it settled against the fabric like it belonged there. Still warm. Still silent. No longer speaking— but reminding. A marker, nothing more. The presence he felt now wasn't from the stone. It was from the shift inside him. The space that had once been hollow was now filled with something he couldn't yet name—but he knew Who it came from.

This was no longer about what had happened in Ilwaco.

It was about what had begun.

And whatever came next, he knew he wouldn't face it alone.

Ben eased himself beneath the covers, the sheets cool against his skin. For the first time in what felt like days, he exhaled without holding anything back. The ache was still there, yes—but it no longer throbbed without aim. It had been given shape. It had been seen. And it had been loved anyway.

He wasn't saying goodbye to Ilwaco.

Some places don't need farewells. They aren't left behind. They follow you—not in distance, but in spirit. They become part of the story you carry, not just the one you remember.

Ben turned off the lamp, pulled the blanket up to his chest, and closed his eyes.

Tomorrow, he would return home and move forward—still unsure what it all meant, still carrying more questions than answers.

But one thing he knew now: he no longer needed the rock.

What he had was something more. Something deeper.

He had witnessed something holy—so real, so alive, that it no longer begged explanation.

The how didn't matter anymore.

He didn't need a relic to remember.

The memory had been sewn into his heart, stitched into the fabric of his soul.

The rock had done its part.

Now, he would carry the truth.

Let it settle.

Let it sting.

Let it speak.

CHAPTER 30

Final Resting Place

The hush of a coastal morning found Ben before dawn. The motel room was cold again, and his back ached from the long night in that narrow bed. But something had settled in him—something he couldn't name. Not peace exactly. Not clarity. Just a stillness that hadn't been there before.

He sat on the edge of the bed, pulled on his jeans and boots, and reached for the jacket draped over the chair. The rock was still in the inside pocket, its shape familiar against his palm. The scarred surface no longer felt mysterious, no longer burned or hummed with unseen weight. It just was. Solid. Present. But not his to carry any longer.

Ben stepped outside, jacket zipped to the collar, the wind tugging softly at the hem. The sky was overcast; the horizon still blurred in gray. The ocean could be heard before it was seen—a long, low breath curling over sand and memory.

He crossed the lot, passed the weathered office, and followed the trail over the dune. The beach opened wide before him—flat, damp, silent. No one else around. Just the waves, the wind, and the footprints he didn't bother leaving behind.

He walked for a while without thinking. The rock heavy in his pocket. Each step unspooling some piece of what he had carried for too long.

Then he saw him.

The old man.

Same layered coat. Same slow gait. Standing near a driftwood log like he'd been waiting—not for anything profound exactly, but for the morning to say what it came to say.

Ben approached without surprise. "Morning," he said, voice hoarse from the cold and whatever else he hadn't spoken.

The old man nodded. "Figured I might see you again."

Ben looked out toward the waves, hands deep in his pockets. "I've been carrying something I can't fully explain. I don't know if it was a vision, a dream, or something divine, but it felt real. More real than anything else I've known."

The old man didn't flinch. "You saw something?"

Ben nodded. "Jesus. The cross. All of it. I was there. Somehow. It wasn't a story anymore. It wasn't metaphor. I saw Him." He paused. "I don't have all the answers, but I know what I saw."

The old man stared out at the sea. "Not everything we see with our eyes is what's real. Sometimes God lets us see with something deeper."

Ben turned toward him. "You really believe that?"

"I do," the man said. "I don't pretend to understand how. Don't need to. God's not small. If He wants to show you something, He can. If He wants to speak, you'll hear it. Not always with your ears. But you'll know."

Ben let that settle.

"I don't think I imagined it," he said softly. "I think God used something simple to show me something holy."

The old man smiled faintly. "That sounds about right."

Ben looked down, pulled the rock from his pocket, cradled it in both hands. "It doesn't feel the same anymore. Not like before."

"That's because it did what it came to do," the man said. "It's not magic. It's a marker. A symbol. You don't have to keep it to keep what it gave you."

Ben nodded slowly. "I think I came here to return it."

"Seems right," the old man said. "Some things aren't meant to be carried forever."

They stood there a moment longer, the waves repeating themselves like Scripture. Then Ben turned and walked toward the water.

He knelt at the place where the tide met the sand—wet, cold, unmoved. He gently placed the rock down, just above the reach of the foam, where the light could still catch its scar. He didn't say a prayer. He didn't need to. He just looked at it for a moment longer, then stood and walked away.

The old man had gone.

Ben didn't look for him. Some things you only see once.

He returned to the motel, packed his bag slowly. Folded the clothes he hadn't worn. Washed the coffee mug. Checked the drawers for anything forgotten. He looked once more at the empty room—its walls, its silence, its worn edges. Then he stepped outside and closed the door.

The drive home was quiet. The sky stayed low, the roads nearly empty. He didn't play music. Didn't rehearse what he'd say or try to frame what he'd seen. He just drove, letting the miles unwind the distance between where he'd been and where he was going.

When he pulled into his driveway, the house looked the same—but it felt different. Not sacred. Not new. Just waiting. Still. The way a place does when it knows the person returning is no longer the same one who left.

He shut off the engine, sat in the quiet for a moment. Then reached for his phone.

A message.

To Claire.

He typed it slowly, thumb resting a beat too long on each word.

We need to talk.

Then he hit send.

And sat there, watching the screen go still, the driveway quiet around him, the story not finished—but finding its way.

The Ending He Knew

Dreams gave way to silence as Ben opened his eyes. Morning sun filtered through the blinds, casting soft golden bars across the hardwood floor. No motel walls. No ocean salt in the air. No musty linens or humming mini-fridge. Just the quiet breath of a house that had waited without judgment.

He moved without rushing. Made coffee. Showered. Pulled on a favorite shirt—the one Claire had once said made him look more rested than he felt. Everything about the morning felt blessedly normal. But beneath the familiar routine, something deeper stirred. Not anxiety nor doubt. Something quieter. Settled. True.

He carried his mug into the office. Same chair. Same desk. But he wasn't the same man who had left this room days ago, uncertain of what he was chasing.

He sat down, took a sip, and looked around the space as if seeing it for the first time: the books, the photos, the soft hum of the monitor waking up. The ache he used to carry in his chest—that constant tension—was gone. Not numbed. Not repressed. Gone.

The rock was no longer with him. He hadn't brought it back from Ilwaco. But he could still see where he'd left it: kneeling in the sand, the tide whispering at the edges, light catching the scar. He hadn't turned back to look. He hadn't needed to. Whatever the rock had once carried—mystery, weight, meaning—it had done its part. What remained wasn't something to hold. It was something to live. A scar, yes—but no longer a wound.

He stared at the blank screen, then whispered, "I know the ending now."

Not the last sentence. Not every word. But the reason. The center. The heart of it.

He still didn't know if what he'd seen in Ilwaco had been supernatural or simply the mercy of God working through imagination. He didn't need to decide. He had seen Jesus. That much was real. The surrender. The love. The mercy. It had been stitched into him.

He picked up his phone. Still no reply from Claire. He'd told her they needed to talk—after everything he'd seen, everything that had unfolded. He wasn't sure what he expected. He only knew he wanted to share it with her.

He set the phone down and moved to the window, watching the breeze ripple across the trees. Made coffee. Stared at the blinking cursor on his laptop without typing a word.

Then, almost an hour later, the screen lit up. A message:

Hi. Nice to hear from you. How have you been?

His chest softened. A quiet smile came. He typed:

Too much to say in a text. Can we meet? Maybe at that place we had dinner a few weeks back?

A minute passed.

Sure. We can meet tomorrow. 5:30 work?

That would be great.

He set the phone down and let the quiet stretch out again. The words weren't finished, but the direction was clear.

He stood fully now and again felt the absence of that old ache. He could still see Jesus in his mind—every detail of the hill, the narrow street, the eyes that had seen through him. The horror still lingered, but so did the love—the unwavering love of the Father in the eyes of the Son.

He sat at the keyboard. His fingers hovered, then moved. Not grasping. Not hesitant. Just ready.

He wrote of scars. Of mercy. Of a Savior Who walked willingly into death with eyes wide open.

He didn't worry about the future with Claire. Didn't obsess over whether the book would be published or sit quietly on a shelf. Those questions no longer held him hostage. Doubts still whispered. Weakness hadn't vanished. But something deeper had settled beneath it all: he was seen. He was loved. And one day—whether soon or far from now—he would stand face to face with Jesus. Not a vision. Not a metaphor. Jesus, real.

He hoped that day was still years away.

Because there was more to write. More to share. He wanted people to know Jesus died for them. That He sees them. Every last one.

The words came freely now, like breath. Like butter across warm bread.

He smiled. Melody would've rolled her eyes at that line. Then laughed.

The day passed. Chapters took shape. As evening neared, he closed his laptop and stepped away. Tomorrow, he'd see Claire. But tonight, he just needed rest.

He didn't know what the next day would hold—not fully. But something was shifting. And this time, he wasn't chasing it. He was ready to receive it.

And the story wasn't over.

CHAPTER 32

The Confirmation

Ben woke early—not from anxiety, but with a kind of settled anticipation. The events of the past few days had reshaped something deep in him—not just his understanding of faith, but of himself. He no longer felt the pressure to explain or justify what he had seen. The visions, if that's what they were, didn't need validation. They had already done their work. He was different now, and he knew it.

After a quiet morning of writing, Ben reached for his phone and sent a message to Mark:

Hey, just wanted you to know I'm nearing the end of the manuscript. Still not sure what I'll do with it, but I want it finished. I've got an ending now. Just need to shape the last few chapters and tighten things up.

He hit send, then leaned back, letting the morning light soak into the room. He felt no urgency. No rush to publish. Just the need to finish something that mattered—not for approval, but for truth.

By late afternoon, he showered, shaved, and dressed simply. There were no expectations for the evening. He wasn't hoping for resolution or romance. He simply looked forward to seeing Claire again—her familiar smile, the sound of her voice. He felt gratitude for her presence in his life, no matter what shape it ultimately took.

The drive to the restaurant was peaceful. The trees lining the highway blurred past, their shadows stretching long in the soft evening sun. Halfway there, he turned off the music, preferring the rhythm of the road, the hush of his thoughts.

As he pulled into the parking lot, he saw Claire's car arriving from the opposite direction. They parked almost in sync and met between their vehicles with the same soft smile of recognition—warm, easy, real.

They hugged—longer than polite, shorter than intimate, but unmistakably sincere.

"Hi," she said.

"Hi," he replied. "You look well."

"So do you."

Inside, they were seated at a quiet booth by the window. Light pooled across the table, softening the edges of everything. The menus sat untouched for a while as they eased into conversation.

"How have you been?" he asked.

Claire exhaled. "Still on pause, I think. But not scared in the same way. I'm not sure I'm ready to move forward, but I'm not afraid of it anymore either."

Ben nodded gently. "That's good to hear."

She tilted her head. "And you? You said there was too much to say in a text. So—what's going on?"

Ben hesitated, then asked, "Would you mind if we prayed first?"

She blinked in surprise, then nodded. "I'd like that."

They bowed their heads, sharing a quiet moment for clarity, presence, peace. When he looked up, Ben began.

"I went back to Ilwaco. I wasn't planning to, but I needed to. And while I was there…I saw something. I don't know if it was a vision, or something else. But it felt real—too real to explain away. I was there at the crucifixion. Not as a symbol. I saw Jesus. And He saw me."

Claire's eyes welled.

"Ben… I've never told anyone this. A year or so after the assault…I had a similar experience. I wasn't asking for it. I didn't even know I needed it. But I saw Him too. On the cross. And in that moment, I knew He saw me. I knew He had carried my pain before I ever lived it. It was…the most real thing I've ever known."

Ben reached across the table, took her hand. "Thank you. I think part of me needed to know it mattered beyond me.

I didn't even realize I was waiting for confirmation until just now."

They sat in silence, the weight of grace between them.

"Maybe that's why we met when we did," Claire whispered. "So you could tell this story. So someone else could feel seen."

Ben nodded. "I don't know the whole picture. But I know I was meant to meet you."

Dinner passed gently. They shifted into lighter conversation—music, meals, how writing seemed to shape time itself. Ben laughed as he said, "Some days it stretches time. Other days it swallows it whole."

Claire smiled. She understood.

When they stepped outside, twilight had softened the sky.

They lingered near their cars.

Claire broke the quiet. "There's still something here between us, but I think we both know the timing isn't right."

Ben nodded. "And that's okay."

"I reached out to Mark," he added. "Told him I'm finishing the book. I'm going to include what I saw—what I experienced. I don't know if it will be published. But it has to be finished."

Claire smiled softly. "I hope it does get published. But even if it doesn't—finish it. And promise me I get to read the final manuscript."

"I promise," he said.

They hugged—one last time, for now. The kind of embrace that says what parting words cannot.

"Take care, Ben Thomas. And don't you dare stop writing."

"Thanks, Claire. Talk soon."

He watched her car disappear down the road, then turned to his own, knowing something sacred had passed between them. He didn't know what came next. But he had a story to finish. And this time, he would.

This time, the road ahead didn't just lead somewhere. It came from something sacred.

He drove into the darkening road ahead—quiet, clear, and alive with purpose.

CHAPTER 33

The Final Stretch

Ben had been writing for hours by the time Mark called.

The sun stood high, casting late morning light across the hardwood floor, when the phone buzzed beside his half-drunk coffee. Words had been coming—not easily, but faithfully. The cursor blinked in the middle of a half-breathed sentence, like it was waiting for the rest to land.

He didn't mind the interruption. He needed it.

"Hey, Mark," he answered, leaning back in his chair.

"You sound buried," Mark said.

Ben chuckled quietly. "That's one word for it. I've been at it since early this morning. This last section's…hard to explain."

Mark's voice softened. "So. The book. You're really going to finish it?"

Ben exhaled, eyes still on the screen. "Yeah. I am. Still don't know if it's meant for shelves or just a shelf in my closet, but I need to finish it. Not perfectly—just honestly."

"I'd love to read it," Mark said. "When do you think we can sit down?"

Ben did the math. "It's Tuesday. Give me till Friday. How's four o'clock at my place?"

"I've got meetings till noon, but that works," Mark replied. "Natalie can't make it; she's got a late consult. You might let Claire know too, in case she was thinking of coming."

Ben's heart caught for a moment. Claire. Her name still landed with weight. Mark didn't know—they were on pause. Not broken. Not bitter. Just…waiting.

"She won't be," Ben said quietly. "We're on pause."

Mark didn't press. "Got it. Looking forward to it."

Ben hung up and stared at the screen. Nothing around him had changed, but something inside him had. He thought of Claire—her voice, the way she smiled. He still felt the ache, soft but persistent, like a note still ringing long after the chord had faded.

He placed his hands back on the keyboard.

This section was the turning point. The place where everything converged—what he'd seen in Ilwaco, what it meant, what it didn't. It wasn't for drama. It wasn't to convince anyone. It was to testify. And it had to be told plainly, with reverence.

He began typing.

The air did not split. There was no thunder. But the world shifted. I was there, and yet I wasn't. I saw Him—not imagined, not symbolic. Jesus. Bloodied. Bent. Carrying what should not have been His to carry. And then, He looked at me.

Ben paused. Then added:

He didn't glance. He saw. Through the noise, the pain, the crowd. He saw my failure, my silence, my shame—and still, He carried it. He chose to.

The words came slow, like a trickle becoming a stream.

He didn't stop typing.

The vision wasn't a rupture in time. It was a reassurance. Not spectacle—grace.

He felt the warmth again. Not from the room. Not from memory. From somewhere deeper. That same pulse that had settled in Ilwaco now stirred quietly beneath his skin.

Then a thought came—subtle, but powerful. He had always known the scar was man-made. But now he understood why. Just as men had scarred Jesus, a man had scarred the rock—to bear witness to the wounds He carried.

There was more to shape. Still chapters to refine. But the heart of the story—the why—it was no longer a question.

He didn't write to be understood. He wrote because he had been seen.

His eyes drifted toward the shelf where the rock had once rested. It was empty. And that was right. It had done its part.

What remained didn't need to be held.

It lived in him now.

CHAPTER 34

What Remains

The next few days passed quickly—some texts from the kids, and more time finalizing the manuscript.

Friday arrived without fanfare. The sky stretched pale and slow, morning clouds draped like gauze across the light.

By the time Mark's car pulled into the drive, Ben had already vacuumed the office, wiped down the counters, and laid two steaks out to thaw. Not from nerves—just readiness. Like setting a stage. Not for performance, but for something real.

He met Mark at the door. A handshake became a hug—easy, familiar, steady.

They moved to the kitchen where iced tea waited on the counter. The air smelled faintly of citrus. Neither of them rushed to say anything of weight. They talked about fishing, work, something dumb from a podcast that made them both laugh harder than expected. But eventually, the conversation tilted.

Mark leaned back, folding his arms. "So…you and Claire?"

Ben didn't answer right away. Not to dodge. Just to breathe. "We're on pause."

Mark nodded. "That's a hard place to sit."

"It is," Ben said. "But it's not resentment. She's not running; she's just being honest about what she needs. And I respect that. I guess I'd rather have something honest that hurts than something comforting that's false."

He paused, fingers brushing his coffee mug.

"Truth is, when someone matters that much, the quiet gets louder when they're not around. But I'd rather wait than force something she's not ready for."

Mark studied him. "You've changed."

"So I've been told," Ben said, half a smile in his voice.

"And the book?"

"I'm close," Ben said. "Still not sure if it's meant to be published. That's not what I'm thinking about today. Today I just want to know if it reads true."

Mark's eyes softened. "Then let's see it."

They moved into the office. Ben handed over the main chair and sat in the second one across the desk, fingers loosely clasped in his lap. Mark started reading around Chapter 7. No small talk. No commentary. Just scrolling—steady, quiet.

Ben watched his face more than the screen. He could tell when something landed—when Mark's brow furrowed, when his lips tightened, when the space between scrolls slowed like he didn't want to leave a paragraph too fast.

Midway through Chapter 11, Mark stopped and leaned back. "Wow."

Ben tilted his head. "Good or bad?"

"Good," Mark said. "Really good. It cut through some fog I didn't know I was carrying."

"Keep going."

Mark did. He read another chapter, then skipped ahead—into one of the deeper, more reflective passages. Ben knew he was getting close to the chapters where he'd written about what happened on the hill. He'd folded it into story form—to let it live within the larger narrative he was telling. With Jesus.

Mark's pace slowed. His posture shifted. At one point, he lifted his hand off the trackpad and just let it hover there.

When he finally stopped, he sat back fully. His eyes were glossy. Not tears. But they'd been close.

"I've read a lot of chapters in my life," he said quietly. "But this? This is something else."

Ben kept his voice low. "Still has rough edges."

"Sure. We'll tighten things. But the heart of it?" He shook his head slightly. "It's sacred. You didn't just describe an event. You immersed the reader in it."

Ben lowered his gaze. "I didn't know if I could do it. If it would hold."

"It holds," Mark said. "It holds and it moves."

He tapped a few keys, then looked back up. "Let's meet next week. Tighten the language here and there. I want Natalie to read it too."

Ben nodded. "I'll have it done by then."

Mark stood and stretched, then reached for Ben's shoulder. "I'm proud of you. Hands down, this manuscript is the most honest, powerful thing you've written."

Ben grinned. "So all my other stuff was junk?"

Mark laughed. "No. Well, maybe. But only because they weren't *this*. They weren't born from this depth. This book has weight."

Mark stepped toward the door, then turned back. "Ben, you were made for story—for truth that lives through fiction. This isn't just a novel. It's something deeper. I've never read anything like it."

Ben let the compliment sit. He wanted to believe it. Maybe he even did. But it still felt strange to hear.

Mark nodded. "And I'll say it again—this needs to go public. It deserves to be read. Don't bury it."

"We'll see," Ben said. "Once it's done—fully done— I'll know."

The door clicked shut behind Mark, and the house fell quiet again.

Ben stayed seated at the desk. The screen in front of him was still—waiting. But the silence around him didn't feel empty. It felt full.

He rested his fingers on the keyboard and began to type.

The final chapter was nearly done.

Just a few more sentences, and it would be complete.

CHAPTER 35

The Call from Home

Ben had just returned from a slow walk—three quiet laps around the block, not for exercise but for clarity. The air held the soft crispness of late afternoon, the kind that hinted at change without announcing it. His footsteps on the sidewalk, the distant hum of a neighbor's lawnmower, the scent of jasmine brushing past his shoulder—all helped shake loose the fog of a long morning spent revising. The manuscript was nearly there. He had tightened Chapter Eleven, rewritten the final lines of the crucifixion vision, and scribbled notes on a few reflections he still didn't know how to frame.

He poured himself a glass of water and stood for a moment at the kitchen sink, the cold glass pressed lightly against his palm. Outside the window, the wind stirred the trees, and the sunlight slanted through the limbs like a benediction. A day like this didn't ask much. Just presence. Just breath.

Then his phone lit up.

Claire.

His chest caught—not painfully, but like the hush that falls in a room just before music starts again. Her name hadn't appeared on his screen in a few days. Not since the last dinner.

He let it ring once more, then answered.

"Hey," he said, voice steady on the outside, though something in him wavered beneath it.

There was a breath on the other end. Then, soft and uncertain: "Hi, Ben. Do you have a minute?"

"Of course. What's going on?"

Claire's voice was quieter than usual. Not distant—just heavy, like she was walking across an emotional bridge that might not hold. "Monica lost a patient yesterday. On the table. Her first."

Ben sat down slowly. "Oh, no. I'm so sorry."

"Yeah." Her voice cracked slightly. "She called me late last night, sobbing. I've never heard her like that. She blamed herself, though it wasn't her fault. She did everything right. The team did everything right. But still..."

He could hear the guilt running through her words like an undercurrent.

"She's devastated, Ben. And I couldn't sleep. I couldn't stop thinking about her being alone with it. So, I booked a flight. I'm going back to Chicago. First thing tomorrow."

"Of course," he said gently. "She needs you."

There was a pause. Not long. Just enough to signal that there was more.

"Ben, there's something else," Claire said. "I'm not sure I'm coming back. I mean—I'll return to get my things, obviously. But...I think I'm moving back—for Monica...and for me."

He didn't respond right away. Just let the words settle, like dust on glass.

"I understand," he said finally. Not because it didn't sting, but because it was true.

"I didn't expect anything," he added. "But some part of me—maybe a hopeful part—did wonder if we'd get another chance."

"So did I," Claire said, and her voice cracked again, just slightly. "And maybe we still will. I don't know. But this... this feels like what I'm supposed to do. I've spent a lot of time trying to rebuild myself, and I think some of that rebuilding needs to happen back there...with her. Maybe with the things I ran from."

Ben steadied himself before he spoke. "I'll certainly be thinking of you."

He leaned forward, elbow resting on his knee, head slightly bowed. "I met with Mark yesterday. We sat down and went through the manuscript. It's almost done now. Just a few sentences left to polish."

"That's amazing, Ben. I'm proud of you."

"I haven't forgotten my promise," he said. "When it's finished, I'll send it to you—whether or not it ever gets published."

"I'd like that," she said softly.

Another pause.

"Ben, you've really touched my life—in ways I didn't expect. You helped me feel seen. Held. And I won't say I'll never see you again—I just know that for now, I need to go home."

Ben closed his eyes for a second, then opened them slowly. "You touched mine too. And I'd be lying if I said I didn't imagine something more. But I'm not going to grip that too tightly. I'll hold it open. Let it be what it is."

Claire gave a soft laugh. "That sounds like another one of your lines."

"Maybe it is," he said. "Maybe it will be."

She sighed. "I should go. I have packing to do. But thank you—for everything. For seeing me. For listening. For being gentle."

"Tell Monica I said hi. I know we've never met, but...I feel like I know a little of her through you."

"I will. Thank you."

There was a silence. Not empty. Not final. Just full.

"Take care, Ben Thomas. And don't you dare stop writing."

"I won't," he said, voice firm through the ache. "Talk to you soon."

The call ended. Ben set the phone down on the table and sat back in his chair.

He wasn't devastated. But he wasn't untouched either. It was the kind of ache that didn't scream; it just lingered. Quiet. Familiar. Like a song that had ended before the final chord.

Some part of him had hoped—if he was honest—that she might show up at his door. That maybe she'd say she was ready. But life didn't always return the echo. Sometimes, it simply moved forward.

He looked toward the desk where his manuscript waited. The story was still alive. Still moving.

And this—whatever it was—would find its way into the pages. Not as closure. But as clarity.

He stood, stretched, and walked to the window. Outside, the wind picked up again, rustling the trees with a sound like applause fading in the distance.

The concert wasn't over. But that last encore had just played its final note.

CHAPTER 36

The Final Touches

The days passed quietly. Not in monotony, but in a steady rhythm that felt almost sacred. Mornings slipped into midday, and evenings arrived like a soft exhale. The occasional call or text from one of his kids helped him breathe.

Ben found himself waking early, but without urgency—making coffee in the silence of the house, the steam curling upward as if it carried something holy. There was peace in the process: tightening the language, trimming the excess, reading old sentences with new eyes, and discovering that some of them still held power.

The manuscript was nearly done.

One morning, he spent hours on Chapter 18, cutting a line that had once felt essential and replacing it with something truer. Then Chapter 19—where Claire had first read his early pages—he sharpened the dialogue, let the silences breathe. The crucifixion scene had already been polished, but he read it again anyway. Not to change it, but to sit with it. The weight still landed. That was enough.

Around midday, his phone rang.

Eric.

Ben smiled as he answered. "Hey, son."

"Hey, Dad. You busy?"

"Just editing. What's up?"

Eric's voice held a warmth that had become familiar lately—like a best friend. "Just checking in. Wondering if you'd want to come out this way sometime soon. Maybe we do some fishing. Nothing fancy. Just hang out. Maybe I finally get to read that manuscript or book you keep hinting about."

Ben leaned back in his chair, smiling. "That sounds good. I'd like that."

He and Eric chatted for a while—about fishing, the weather, and a new show. Nothing deep, but it didn't need to be. It was good just to connect. When they hung up, Ben sat quietly for a moment, the phone still in his hand. Not because anything had changed—but because he was grateful. For the simplicity. For the constancy.

Later, a message lit up his phone. Claire.

Chicago seems so big now. Monica's doing okay. She's tired but hanging in there. Thank you for the prayers—really.

Ben read the text slowly. He smiled—not because it fixed anything, but because it mattered. She didn't owe him a message. But she'd sent one anyway.

He typed back: *You've been on my mind. Praying for both of you.*

He stared at the screen a little longer, then set the phone aside and turned back to his desk. He finished reading the final pages of the manuscript. The lines were starting to blur, but the message felt clear. He knew there would be tweaks still to come—but for now, the manuscript was ready.

That night, Mark called.

"Hey," Mark said. "Natalie and I were talking—we'd love to read what you've got. How about dinner at our place? Bring your laptop, we'll cook, and then go over it together."

Ben hesitated, then smiled. "Actually, I was thinking I'd send you the final manuscript as a PDF tonight. That way, you and Natalie can take your time. Read it through. Then we can talk."

Mark paused. "It's finished?"

"It's finished. Or as close as it's going to get for now."

"Send it. I'm excited."

After they hung up, Ben sat down at his desk, did one last pass through the final chapter, then exported the file. He attached it to an email with a short note:

Here it is. No pressure. Just truth.

He clicked send.

Then he closed the laptop and sat back, staring out the window at the trees swaying gently in the late afternoon breeze. He felt a hum beneath his ribs—not nerves. Not fear. Something else.

Expectation.

He didn't know what Mark and Natalie would say. He didn't know if the book would ever find a wider audience or not. But he knew it was honest. And for the first time since he began this journey, he wasn't afraid to let it be seen.

He was ready.

Not just to finish.

But to release.

CHAPTER 37

Before the Verdict

The next morning, Ben woke up feeling a little unmoored. No manuscript to chase. No new chapter waiting. Just stillness—and waiting for whatever came next.

He made coffee, poured a cup, and stepped out onto the deck. The air was fresh, crisp in a way that made the world feel new. Birds sang—melodies of songs long forgotten, and maybe some not yet sung.

He thought back to the old man in Ilwaco. Wondered what he'd asked God that day. Then wondered—*what should I be asking?*

Ben didn't expect the text to hit the way it did when it arrived:

Mark: *Got the file. Just reread the first couple chapters. Man, it pulls you in even stronger the second time. Looking* *forward to going all the way through. How about we meet in two days, Thursday? Our place, 5:30. I've got some fresh salmon you're going to love. I've been working on a new preparation—Natalie says it might be my best yet.*

Ben smiled at the screen, already imagining the scent of garlic and rosemary, the warmth of their kitchen, the sound of Natalie laughing at Mark's latest culinary invention. Mark was a serious cook—precision without pretense—and every dinner invitation was a guaranteed highlight. This one, though, would carry more. The weight of a finished story. A full read. And whatever came next.

Over the following days, Mark sent a few more texts, each one drawing Ben closer to something that now felt bigger than both of them.

Mark (Tuesday, 11:47 a.m.): *Hard to put this manuscript down, brother. Really.*

Mark (Wednesday, 3:13 p.m.): *Already halfway through. Might finish tonight.*

Mark (Wednesday, 9:42 p.m.): *Natalie says it's your best. By far. See you tomorrow.*

Ben read each message slowly, letting the encouragement reach the places where doubt still lingered. He didn't need validation—but it helped. Especially from people who understood story structure as well as Mark and Natalie. Especially from someone who knew him.

Later that night, he texted Claire, forgetting the time difference.

Ben: *Just checking in. How are you two holding up?*

She didn't respond right away. He wasn't sure she would.

A quiet buzz pulled him from his notes.

Claire: *Things are settling down. Monica's still processing, but she's doing better. She's strong. I shared some things with her I hadn't before—about what I saw. About what you saw too. It comforted her more than I expected. Thank you.*

Ben read the message twice. Then once more.

The rest of the night passed quietly.

Later, he sat on the deck with a glass of water in hand, the stars soft and scattered above him. The air had cooled—the kind of calm that made you forget how loud the world could be. He wasn't nervous. Not really. Just present. Aware that tomorrow held something meaningful.

Not an ending. Not even a beginning.

Just a quiet affirmation that his life hadn't been wasted.

That the ache, the questions, the pages—they all mattered.

CHAPTER 38

Give It Time

Thursday evening had finally arrived.

Ben stood by the window, watching the sky shift through pale blues and soft golds. A quiet calm had settled over the day—the kind that didn't need explaining. That morning he'd looked through the manuscript one last time, not to revise it, but out of reverence. The work was finished. Now came the verdict.

He checked the time. Just after four.

He pulled out his phone and typed a message to Claire:

Hey—heading over to Mark and Natalie's in a bit. They've read the manuscript. Tonight's the night I get their verdict. Just wanted to let you know. Been thinking of you.

He hesitated before hitting send. No expectations—just a simple truth.

Her reply came a few minutes later:

Thank you for telling me. I'm sure it's beautiful, Ben. I'll be praying for peace, no matter what they say. And yes…I've been thinking of you too.

Ben sat with that for a moment.

Then he stood, ran a comb through his hair, and buttoned his shirt slowly. He wasn't dressing for an event. He was dressing for something closer to sacred—a meal with two friends who had walked beside him quietly, faithfully, through the birth of a book that might never leave the circle of those who knew him best. And yet, it meant everything.

The drive was uneventful, but his thoughts flickered like headlights on a rain-slick road. Images rose up—pre-dawn writing sessions, the scarred rock, Claire's eyes, the motel room in Ilwaco. There was no single thread. Just the strange, holy weave of it all. The nights that broke him. The mornings that stitched him back together.

By the time he pulled up to Mark and Natalie's house, the sky had deepened into amber. He turned off the engine, took a breath, and stepped out. The scent of grilled fish already floated in the air.

Mark met him at the door with a wide grin and a hug that didn't ask permission. Natalie appeared behind him, wiping her hands on a towel, her smile carrying something gentle and unspoken.

"Come on in," she said. "We've been looking forward to this."

Ben stepped inside, heart steady but expectant. Tonight wasn't about perfection. It wasn't about publication. It was about truth—and whether it had landed.

He hoped it had.

And he was ready to find out.

They talked for a while—about life, the weather, the strange quiet that had settled over everything lately. Nothing forced. Nothing heavy. Just honest conversation between old friends who had learned not to rush meaning.

Eventually, Mark leaned back, folded his hands across his stomach, and said, "This won't come as a shock—I haven't exactly been quiet about how I feel. But now that we've read every word—Natalie and I both—I can say it with confidence: it's strong, Ben. Really strong. It feels nearly complete."

He glanced at Natalie, then added, "She had a few light notes—just small things, a smoother line here or there. Nothing that would take more than a couple days."

He paused. "I really think you've got something here."

Before Ben could respond, Mark stood with a flash of urgency. "Oh—the fish! I nearly forgot." He disappeared into the kitchen.

Natalie smiled and shook her head. "He's worse than a kid when he gets into his recipes."

She turned to Ben, her tone softer now. "Hey...I know it's not my place, and I don't mean to pry. But don't give up on Claire yet."

Ben looked down and nodded once. "Thank you. But… she's planning to stay in Chicago. That's what she told me."

Natalie tilted her head. "Yes, I know. But I'm not convinced that's what her heart wants. She likes you, Ben. I think it's written all over her face when she talks about you."

"I like her too," he said quietly. "But I'm not going to pull her away from her daughter. I can't imagine being that far from my kids—not if they needed me."

Natalie nodded. "I think she just needs time. She's a momma with a hurting child. Give her grace."

"I'm not holding my breath," Ben said, a faint smile at the corner of his mouth. "But I'm not shutting the door either."

They let the topic settle as Mark returned, a triumphant look on his face. "Dinner's ready. You're going to love this—new recipe. I'm telling you, this salmon's going to make you forget every other meal you've had."

They moved to the table, and the evening unfolded with laughter, good food, and talk that wandered from music to memories to favorite old books. As they ate, Mark leaned in again, more serious now.

"I mean it, Ben. This book isn't just personal; it's powerful. It's got a heartbeat. I think it's publication material. And if you'd let me, I'd like to move this story forward. Get our design team on it. We could have the layout cleaned up, a cover mocked up, the whole thing ready for print in two weeks."

Ben sat back, the weight of it pressing in—not heavy, just real. "I'll need to think on it," he said.

Mark smiled. "Of course. But I'm telling you—it's that tight. Not much more needed to make it a work of art."

Later, as the plates cleared and the air grew quieter, Ben thanked them both and stepped toward the door. Mark followed, holding it open.

Ben stepped onto the porch, paused, then turned back. "Two weeks, you think?"

Mark nodded, certain. "Easily. We could be holding a finished paperback copy in our hands in a month or so."

Ben looked out at the fading light, then back at his friend. "You know what? I think I'm ready. Let's do it."

Mark grinned and clapped a hand to Ben's shoulder. "That's what I was hoping to hear."

Ben smiled, stepped down the porch steps, and walked to his car—as if a quiet weight had lifted.

A decision had been made. The pages that had once been private were now stepping out into the world.

It was time.

CHAPTER 39

Ben's Story

Ben's drive home was quiet—the kind of quiet that doesn't ask for music. Dusk trailed behind him as he pulled into the driveway, headlights washing across the porch like a final curtain drawn on a long act. Mark and Natalie's voices still echoed—not just encouragement, but something deeper: the affirmation that this story mattered. Not just because it was his, but because it was true.

Inside, the house greeted him with silence. No sense of absence. No longing. Just stillness. A place that had waited for him to return, changed.

He texted Claire:

Well, they liked it. I agreed to publish.

Her response came almost instantly:

I'm beyond thrilled for you. I can't wait to see it.

Ben smiled. He typed back:

About a month, they said. Then I'll be holding it in my hands.

I'll be praying it lands in the right ones, she wrote.

The days moved quickly. Cover designs. Final read-throughs. The manuscript grew more familiar each time, but also more sacred. He wasn't editing now. He was bearing witness to what had already been given.

Claire had messaged once or twice in the weeks after that text. Kind words. Gratitude. A brief update about Monica's recovery. After that, the thread went quiet.

Ben didn't take it personally. Not everything needed a conclusion. Some connections weren't broken—they were simply still.

Then the books arrived.

A simple box on the porch. Unopened at first. He sat beside it, resting his palms on the top, whispering thanks without words. Then he opened it—slowly. Inside: clean matte covers, crisp pages. The story, bound. Not for fame. Not for noise. Just told.

He sent a message to Claire:

The books came today.

No reply. He didn't expect one right away.

He texted Mark too. Mark answered quickly, full of celebration and belief.

Evening fell.

Ben read through the crucifixion chapter again, this time not as a writer, not even as a man looking for answers. Just as a witness. The page glowed faintly in the lamplight. Not from the paper. From what it contained.

Then—a knock at the door.

Ben stood, breath pausing. He opened it.

Claire.

She didn't say anything at first. Just smiled gently, eyes full but calm.

Ben blinked. "You're here."

She nodded. "Got in last night. Just for a day or two. Monica's doing better. I needed to come."

He stepped aside, and she entered like someone who didn't need to ask permission.

As they sat, Ben glanced once at her phone still in her hand. Part of him had wondered all day if she'd ever reply. But now, with her here, the silence made a strange kind of sense.

Finally, she looked at him. "I came back," she said. "Not for answers. Not even for closure. I came to see what you made."

Ben nodded. He handed her a copy of the book.

She turned it in her hands like it might warm her fingers.

"Something stirred," she said. "Not longing. Not regret. Just...a knowing. That this story—it's not just yours. It's ours. Mine. Anyone who's ever carried something scarred and called it holy."

Ben swallowed the ache rising in his chest. "It wasn't about writing a book anymore. Somewhere along the way, it became about surrendering to what needed to be said."

Claire opened the book to the chapter titled *The Hill Called Skull.* Her fingers paused on the title.

She looked up, voice quiet. "This is where it happened, isn't it?"

Ben nodded slowly. "And I'll never be the same."

Claire closed the book and held it to her chest—not like a possession, but a gift.

"Thank you," she said. "For telling it. For not softening the truth. For carrying it all the way home."

Ben exhaled. The room felt full—not with tension, not with unfinished love—but with peace.

Claire stood to go. "I won't stay long. Just wanted to see it with my own eyes."

Ben walked her to the door.

"Will you keep in touch?" he asked.

"I think we both will," she said. "In the ways that matter."

They embraced—not romantic, not restrained. Just real.

When the door closed behind her, Ben stood for a long moment, holding the book in his hand.

The scar on the rock. The weight of the cross. The stillness of the ocean. The silence after surrender.

This was the story.

Not just the one he wrote.

The one he lived.

"Who is Tommy Turner?"

I'm not a pastor. I'm not a theologian. I'm just a man who's lived long enough to know what regret feels like—and what grace feels like too.

I've spent years tuning pianos and trading stocks. I've made mistakes. I've wasted time. I've waited for things that never came. But I've also walked the coastline, journal in hand, asking God: *Is there still something for me?* And over time, I've come to believe the answer is yes.

I write faith-based fiction rooted in the coastal towns I've visited—stories that explore how God speaks quietly through memory, beauty, pain, and presence. I don't write sermons. I write stories—because sometimes, a story is what it takes to help someone believe again. Through every character, every page, every setting, I'm saying: You are called. You are not disqualified. Your purpose is not finished.

– Tommy Turner

To learn more visit us on the web: tommyturner.com

www.ingramcontent.com/pod-product-compliance
Lightning Source LLC
Chambersburg PA
CBHW060712190726
48289CB00002B/653